This Ain't What You Run Fo

Stories

Eric S. Piotrow[...]

Copyright © 2013 by Eric S. Piotrowski

All rights reserved.

ISBN: 1-490-51778-2
ISBN-13: 978-1-490-51778-0

Justified Textworks
www.just-text.org

No book was ever worth the writing that wasn't done with the attitude that 'this ain't what you rung for, Jack—but it's what you're damned well getting'.

Nelson Algren
Nonconformity
c. 1950

Contents

Agoraphobia	7
z	37
Respawn	91
Kr Services, LLC	115
Lost Track	135
Imposition	153
The Fiction Journal 31 Shorties	203
Letter to a Young Writer	253
Gratitude	263

Agoraphobia

for Mark

Agoraphobia: Anxiety about being in places or situations from which escape might be difficult (or embarrassing) or in which help may not be available. [...] The situations are avoided (e.g., travel is restricted) or else are endured with marked distress [...] or require the presence of a companion.

Diagnostic and Statistical Manual of Mental Disorders Fourth Edition (DSM-IV)

Most of the women in your life had their heads down. [...] It is not shame, however, that kept their heads down. They were singing, searching for meaning in the dust. And sometimes, they were talking to faces across the ages, faces like yours and mine.

Edwidge Danticat
"Women Like Us"

July 2010

Maria hesitated and muttered "I gotta go" and hung up the phone. A second later the door splintered and exploded and two cops stormed into the tiny hotel room, guns drawn.

"Police! Get down on the—" But Maria was face-down on the floor, hands behind. One of them stood over her and pulled out the steel cuffs. "Thought you could hide, Gonzales," he said. He snapped them on, tight, and pulled her up. She winced, and he noticed she was talking to herself. He jostled her. "What?"

She moved into a whisper. He could only catch the occasional word: "..today.. myself..". The cop rolled his eyes and pushed her toward his partner.

"You take her," he said. His partner nodded and guided Maria out into the hallway. Some of the people in nearby rooms watched through tiny cracks. They went to the stairs, and then down into the street. He looked up to make sure the light in the room was still on, and then produced his key and loosened the cuffs. He pushed her gently into the back of the cruiser. Three people stood nearby, watching.

The officer got behind the wheel and started it up. "I heard about your husband," he said. "I understand why you did it." The engine hummed. "Why didn't you use an alias?" He looked at her in the rearview. She shook her head. His partner appeared and got in.

Maria gazed out the window as they left the hotel parking lot. She mumbled a string of words he couldn't hear, but eventually said, a little louder: "He deserved to die."

"Maybe they'll go easy on you," the driver said.

"I hope not," his partner said, glancing back at her. "Psycho girl." He chuckled. "Last thing my wife needs is getting ideas like that." He turned to the driver. "You know she stabbed him in the crotch?" The driver nodded slowly, and his partner glanced back at Maria. "What a psycho," he said.

Maria's voice continued, a low murmur beneath the hum of the engine and the occasional crackle of dispatch. She spoke up a little: "I deserve to be punished for what I did."

The second cop nodded. "Got that right," he said. The driver sighed.

1992

I am ten years old. My mother is furious, she is screaming at me. This is not a new thing; in fact I have gotten used to it. I didn't wash the dishes after school so now I'm paying the price. She uses horrible words and gestures angrily at me while she slams frozen processed food into the microwave and sets it going.

My sister is terrified. She stands beside me, quivering, as our mother yells at me and calls me names. The yelling and the names seep into our minds and keep us awake at night. I have nightmares all the time. I lie awake in the dark and doubt myself and wonder if I'll ever really sleep again.

The yelling gets louder. My sister doesn't know what to do, but I do. I stand a little in front of her, ready to be a shield in case things get worse. Our mother has never hit us, but I won't be surprised if she does, one day soon. Our last mother did.

I know what to do, because I've been here before. Once when my sister was staying late at school, taking a test, I got it alone. The insults, the cursing, the yelling. She blames me for her boyfriend leaving, but of course that happened before we showed up. She blames me for her headaches and insomnia, but of course the drinks are probably responsible. She blames me for not doing the dishes, and she's right. It all becomes one moment; the fluid movement of time stagnates and it happens once, together.

Laura holds my hand weakly; she does not want our mother to see. The yelling goes on, we wait. I am only a little older than my sister, but I feel the weight of protection. I hear her whimpering. I can't do anything about it. Or maybe I can.

"If I talk like this," I say to her, in a voice next to silence, "can you hear me?"

"Yes," my sister says.

"Then I'll talk like this."

And so it begins. My words are cloaked in shadow, impossible to see. Sneaking in the hollows between the rage, dropping in between syllables, heard only by my sister.

I tell her that we will be okay. I tell her that our mother is wrong. I tell her that I will always be there to protect her. I tell her that this, too, shall pass. I tell her that people who do bad things experience bad things. Only one of these do I believe with any certainty.

April 2012

Maria dribbled, posted up near the corner, and shot the ball. It hit the backboard and sank in. She said something quietly about having game. She retrieved the ball and dribbled slowly, speaking softly to herself. As usual, she was alone on the court. The other women lifted weights, stood around smoking cigarettes.

A tall woman with short braids appeared and snatched the ball from her hands. "What is your problem?" she asked.

Maria took a step back and lowered her head, glaring at the woman with eyebrows of suspicion. She spoke quietly. "What do you mean?"

"You're always talking to yourself," the woman said. "Always babbling and muttering and stuff. It's creepy as hell."

A guard near the fence waved at them. "Jackie, leave that girl alone."

Jackie waved. "It's all right, man," she said. "We just talkin'." She froze and swung her gaze back toward Maria. "You had something to do with that fire the other day, didn't you?"

Maria blinked, but didn't change her eyes. "What fire?"

Jackie dropped her voice. "Don't play me stupid," she said. "You're a damn freak, and freaks are the ones who do stuff like start fires."

Maria blinked at her again. "My mother told me not to play with fire." She reached for the ball. "You could get hurt."

Jackie pulled the ball back. "My girl Yvette's next to you in cell block four." She narrowed her eyes. "She said she heard you talking to yourself extra angry when the fire broke out."

"Fire makes me nervous," Maria said. "I was scared someone was hurt."

"Yeah," Jackie said. "And you don't want no one gettin' hurt, do you?" She dribbled the ball and went to the corner and took a shot. "Just your husband." She retrieved the ball and passed it to Maria. "I heard you stabbed him in the nuts."

Maria said a few words under her breath, dribbled, and took a shot from three. It sank in clean. Jackie grabbed the ball and went to the same spot. She paused, lining up her shot. "He hit ya?"

Maria nodded a little, whispered something inaudible. Jackie took the shot and it clattered against the backboard and dropped in. She got the ball and gave it to Maria, who took a shot and missed. Jackie made a free throw and passed to Maria. Maria muttered something about Epiphany Prince and sank her shot.

A few minutes later Jackie missed another shot and cursed. She pulled a pack of cigarettes from her pocket and tossed them to Maria. She caught them and gave Jackie a puzzled look.

Jackie smiled. "You didn't know we were playing Horse?" Maria's face softened and she said something. Jackie shook her head. "You should pay more attention," she said, and took the ball back. "But I was sure you would owe me," she said, dropping a shot. "I watched you last week and you were bricking like crazy." She grabbed the ball and dribbled.

Then she stopped and looked sideways at Maria. "Were you hustling me?"

Maria pulled a smoke out and lit it. She smiled. "Sort of."

1999

I can't even remember his name. That's how stupid this whole thing is. I am in bed with him, we're both sweating. My sister throws the door open; I curse and stop moving. She stands there, her duffel bag pulling her body to the right, the dark green hoodie sweatshirt unzipped. She's let her hair grow out; I've been keeping mine short. She is a silhouette in the light from the hallway. She's supposed to be in Chicago. But she's not; she's here, and we're busted. I should apologize and beg for her forgiveness, but I don't. I get indignant as I get dressed. Her boyfriend wasn't worth it anyway. She's standing there, muttering something about how she thought she could trust me.

I try to think of what I can say, and before I know it I'm talking to myself too. We're both like crazy people, spewing weird streams of words. The odd thing is that the words wriggle between each other; they don't clash or bump into themselves. Even while I call her hideous names and blame her for not satisfying her man, my voice seeps into hers and together we sound like one person speaking with great speed.

We get louder. The guy — such a scumbag — he's just laughing. She's such a stupid little girl for getting with him in the first place, and I am even littler and stupider for cheating with him. What the hell do I know? I'm seventeen. He's twenty something. He meets her at a party in Brooklyn, they hook up right away. He knows exactly what he's doing, but we have no idea. We won't know, for years. Maybe we'll never know.

I think back to that time when I didn't do the dishes. I was in the wrong then, and I'm in the wrong now. But some weird sense of pride throws itself up into my brain and I can't back down. Something about always being on the defensive — you lose the ability to tell when you actually *are* wrong. But I deserve better than this. She owes me.. something. It's ludicrous, but it clouds my mind and instead of doing what I ought to do, I do what I want to do.

Her words get louder and slower. "I loved you," she says. "This kind of betrayal.. I just don't understand it."

I say something nasty and biting, about how she's put on weight. It's stupid, something a child would say. Well, I guess that makes sense. She's crying now, and I realize she hadn't been crying this whole time.

But I have. I'm angry at her, but of course I'm really angry at myself.

"I'll never forgive you for this," she says.

"Good," I spit back. "I don't want you to." And I don't. I grab my stuff from the table and head for the door. The guy's still in bed, smiling, smoking a cigarette, watching it all go down. He couldn't care less about either of us.

"I hope you die," she says, quietly, just as I get next to her. He can't hear her.

"You know what?" I spit back, furious. I sound like my mother with the yelling. "Don't just hope." I point to her face, even though I'm right beside her. I've always been right beside her. I'm talking louder than I should be. My words are jagged; they feel wrong in my mouth but they're moving on their own and I have no control over them. "I'm dead." I step back. "There, Maria, I said it. Go and be happy with your stupid boy here." I spit toward the bed, and the guy laughs. "I'm going where you should have been."

I slam the door on my way out.

April 2012

The guard banged a stick on the bars and the clang reverberated off the walls of the cell. Maria mumbled something quietly and looked up. His keys jangled and he shook his head. "Hey Sybil," he said. "You got a visitor."

Maria rose and pulled her arms together. She whispered something about love and gratitude and the noise and the silence, and followed the guard out into the hallway.

She felt her eyes get wet as she spotted Sebastian, sitting there in the room full of small chairs and wobbly tables. She could see the hospital scrubs under his jacket. To his right a father joked around with his sons. Sebastian looked up and their eyes met and he waved a little.

Maria approached and paused for a moment as he stood up. She started crying a little and Sebastian scowled. "You okay?" he asked.

She nodded and smiled through her tears. She hugged him, tight. "It's so good to see you," she said. He hugged her back.

"Must have been a rough week," he said.

She held on. "Yeah," she said. "Pretty rough." She reached into the back of his jacket and dropped something into the little pocket near his neck. "This is the last one," she whispered.

He pulled away. "Why?"

"She's getting better," Maria said as they sat down. "I don't need to keep sending them."

Sebastian nodded, but his face was full of worry. "I was talking to a shrink that works with some of the kids," he said. "I asked him and he said maybe your mom's got agoraphobia."

Maria thought back to the library. It was warm there, a good place to go during the day when she was on her own. When she started to think she was losing it, she'd read up on some different mental problems. "Is that the one where you always worry you're going to get raped?"

He shook his head. "No, it's about being scared to go outside." He sat back and his mini-dreadlocks bounced a little. "He said her condition pretty much fits the description."

Maria shrugged. "Could be," she said. "But she says she's doing fine these days. She's going to church all the time." He let out a slow breath. "Seriously," she said. "I know you're worried, but .. trust me. She'll be okay."

"I wish I could meet her," he said. "Just to make sure there's nothing.. you know, physical. Just check her pulse and stuff."

Maria smiled and squeezed his hand. "I know," she said. "But trust me. I know this woman. She's doing okay." A moment passed. She dropped her head a little to make eye contact. "Trust me."

He nodded. "Okay."

2001

I meet Sebastian at the June parade in East Harlem. I'm totally hot for him — his copper skin is vibrating with the drums. But his girl just died from breast cancer and suddenly I'm a skank for even thinking about it. Within a month I realize I would have made a crazy mistake anyway. He's way too conservative and quiet and timid. Still, he knows how to listen to a girl and he knows what he wants. Late one night when we're hanging out on the roof of his apartment building, he makes it clear that what he wants isn't me. I feel hurt for about a week, and then I realize I'm being stupid and I get over it and I go back to appreciating how lucky I am to have a friend like him.

He asks to meet my mom, but I explain how she's scared of everyone. I feel bad because I want to have him over, but it's just not possible. I can't let him that far into my life. Maybe in a few years. I've met his brother and his aunt, and I feel like I'm being weird. But he understands. He gives me space.

In August he takes me to a party in The Bronx. There are too many people, the music's too loud, too much debauchery. Sebastian is uncomfortable but we dance a little anyway. When he steps away for half a second, Alexander is there.

Alexander is strong — he works out while Sebastian is watching TV shows about cooking. Alexander is wild, driven. He moves like he's trying to keep his center of gravity low, his legs writhing with a ferocious sensuality. I pretend to be unimpressed. He can tell I'm faking. We dance. Before I know it, we're kissing in a dark corner. I find Sebastian and tell him I'm going home with Alexander.

He raises an eyebrow. "That guy?" he asks.

I tilt my head. "C'mon, Seb. Let a girl have some fun."

He hugs me. "Okay, but just.. be careful."

I smile. "I will."

Twenty minutes later he's tearing through the borough, way over the speed limit. It's the most exciting thing to happen to me in three years. I want more. I tell him to go faster, speaking in a low murmur. He realizes a cop is chasing us and he decides to lose him. Sharp turns and quick stops and suddenly we're in a parking garage and we can hear the cop tear past. We start kissing.

One month later he brings me up onto the roof of his apartment building. I can see Sebastian's place. Alexander and I see each other every day. He waits for me after work. Today he wants to show me something.

"Here," he says, handing me his cell phone. I take it, confused.

He produces another one. It's red. He brings up the contact list and shows it to me. All females — Angie, Carmen, Celestina, Eva, Isabel, Monique, Zoe. He takes it back and presses some buttons. A delete confirmation pops up.

"You push it," he says. It's silly but it feels good anyway. After I push it he takes a step back and then throws the red phone as far as he can. Then he kisses me and then he pulls out a box and before I know what's happening he's on his knee and there's a half-carat of diamonds staring at me. I whisper a prayer of thanks.

"Maria—"

I say yes before he even asks.

April 2012

Sebastian stepped off the bus and crossed the street. He went into the lobby of the rundown brick building and approached the mailboxes. Trash and junk mail decorated the room; he could smell urine. He gazed at the mailbox marked "Santiago", then produced the flash drive and slid it through the slot. It clattered to the bottom and he glanced around.

The door to a maintenance closet stood ajar. He glanced down the hallway toward the first-floor apartments, then up the narrow staircase. No one. Cheap yellow paint over splintered woodwork. He went into the closet and turned on the light. A desk with a folding chair, two brooms, and a plunger. He turned the light off and closed the door most of the way. He could see the mailboxes through the opening. He pulled the folding chair around and sat.

He waited.

2005

It doesn't take long for the honeymoon to end. I should have seen it coming. Six years later but I'm still that stupid girl, chasing thrills and pretending to be invincible. He's yelling at me now, insane with jealousy.

"Didn't I cut all of them off for you?" he asks, waving his hand upward. Same spot where he threw his ladies' phone away. Same spot he threatened to push me off last week.

"Sebastian's just a friend," I say, and drink. He drinks and stares at me. The window is open; it's hot. I can tell he's close to passing out. Wish he'd just hurry up and do it.

"No such thing," Alexander says. "Friendzone now, but he's just waiting."

I roll my eyes. He seethes, tries to stand up. He falls over and crawls to the garbage can and vomits into it and spits on the ground. "Look at what you're doing to me," he says. Quietly — he's muttering.

"You're doing it to yourself," I say, but I wonder if maybe he's right. Do I even know what I want? He's given me a good home, bought me a car. He wants kids but I just don't know. He's willing to hit me; why would he be different with them?

It's never anything bad. I'll throw something and he'll throw something and we'll both yell and someone gets hurt. Not hurt bad, just a little hurt. He gets hurt emotionally, I get hurt physically. It's all pain.

Of course that's only during the bad times. There are plenty of good times. Flowers and forgiveness, the confessions of fear, the baring of souls. Promises, protection, pride.

He passes out and I go out. Just walking for a while, and then over to Sebastian's. We go up on his roof and talk. I steer clear of anything serious. He tells me about the latest girlfriend. His voice is getting a little desperate. I think he's changed his mind about me, but I can't really tell.

There's a silence and I start singing, nearly a whisper. Something we used to sing in school. It's reassuring. Eventually it becomes a string of words. Sebastian is peering at me.

"What?" he asks.

I make the words come together more. ".. can't keep going.. hate myself.." I'm crying and he holds my hand. ".. ribs .. he knows how to not leave a mark.." A siren comes and goes.

He sighs and nods slowly. "How long has it been going on?"

I shrug a little and let more words flop around. ".. about a year.. gets better, then not.."

"Why don't you leave him?" he asks.

I look up, tears smearing my dark eyes. *And marry you instead?* I wipe my eyes. "I still love him," I say.

One hour later I'm back home. He's managed to make it into bed. I sit down on it and untie my shoes. He pushes himself beside me and wraps an arm around my waist. "I'm so sorry," he says, groggy. He sniffles and does a little sob into my back. I can never tell if it's real or not. "I just get so scared."

I roll my eyes and pull the shoes off. He falls in a way that lets him look right up at me.

"If you left me, I'd kill myself."

I look away.

April 2012

Sebastian shifted his weight again and yawned. Two hours and three false alarms. On the bright side, none of them seemed to notice him. He wondered how a person became a private investigator. He also wondered what he was going to eat for dinner. Hunger was starting to gnaw at him.

Then she appeared. Baseball cap, dark green hoodie sweatshirt. Sunglasses. Black jeans, black sneakers. *She's way too young to be her mother.* Right to the Santiago mailbox, key out. Opened it, grabbed the drive, closed it, locked it. *Should I jump out and say something?*

She walked out the front door and Sebastian checked his watch. Another hour of daylight. He waited a few seconds, then left the closet. He went into the street and saw her turn the corner. He zipped up his jacket and went after her.

2010

I'm standing in the kitchen. There's silverware all over the floor. Broken glass, various fluids. One of his shoes came off at some point. My hands are shaking. I'm talking to myself.

"What happened? What happened? Who is it? Who am I?" I look around. I'm seeing red. Lots of red, all over. He wanted me. "I didn't want him. He didn't care what time of the month it was." I sit down and my jeans are instantly soaked. "I'm bleeding." I look at my hands. I'm seeing red. "I'm seeing red," I say. Just putting words out there.

He can't hear me now.

"He never heard me. Well if he did, he didn't listen." I look at him. "You never listened." He just looks up at the ceiling. Well, sort of. I chuckle a little. "Your phone was red," I say. "Everything's red."

I stand up and change into different jeans. I pull on my dark green hoodie and grab my keys. Then I put the keys down and go and wash my hands. I go where the floor is clean and put on my shoes and then wrap some plastic bags around them. I put a bag on my hand. "Can't get caught red-handed," I say. My voice is low, next to silence. "He's like Laura now," I say. I wonder where she is.

I have to get out of the city. I pull the car key off the ring and leave the apartment. I drive west. The GPS talks to me and I talk to it.

Later I roll down the window. "Sorry, GPS," I say. "I can't risk it." I throw it off the bridge and keep going west.

April 2012

Sebastian unzipped his jacket. It was warm in the library. The magazines were beside the checkout counter.

Agoraphobia

He grabbed a sports weekly and flipped through it. Not very busy, but enough people to hide him. He thought about a video game he'd played once where he had to sneak around by standing in groups of people. This felt about the same.

She sat down at a computer and pulled off her sunglasses and glanced around. She pulled out the flash drive and put it in, then clicked the mouse a few times. She pulled a pair of earbuds out of her pocket and plugged them in. She put one in her ear and dropped her head a little and closed her eyes.

No sense waiting around, he thought. He walked to her and tapped her on the shoulder. "Excuse me, miss—"

She spun around and pulled the earbud out. He could hear a few words: ".. one of us should be happy.." She smiled.

He stepped back, his eyes wide. "What the hell!?" Some of the people at other computers looked up at him, then away.

"Quiet." She pulled the flash drive out and hit alt-F4 several times and all the windows vanished and she pulled out the earbuds and stuffed them into her pocket.

"Maria, what the f—"

"Shhh!" She put a finger to her lips and stood up. "C'mon."

They went outside and she hailed a cab. He felt numb. They got in.

"Hoboken," she said. The driver nodded and headed west.

2010

I'm hungry. The sun is going down and I haven't eaten all day. I'm sitting under a bridge and staring into the disgusting water. I'm muttering to myself about how lucky the fish are, and then I look up and Laura's there.

I freeze and I am silent.

"How did you get here?" I ask.

She smiles. "I have my ways," she says, and hands me a bag. I open it and pull out a cheeseburger and fries and I inhale them. She sits on the ground beside me.

"Thanks," I say. I crumple the bag into a tight ball and throw it in the river. I wipe my hands on my dark green hoodie.

A few minutes go by. I want to say something but everything seems useless. Finally I hear her sniffle and she rubs her nose.

"If I talk like this," she says, in a voice next to silence, "can you hear me?"

I start crying. "Yes."

"You killed him."

"Yes."

"They're looking for you."

"I know."

Some silence.

"He hit you."

"Yes." I cry. "And raped me."

She reaches over and takes my hand. "I'm sorry," she says.

I nod, but she pushes my head to face her.

"I'm sorry," she says again, so quiet I can barely hear her. But I can. I hear her perfectly. "For everything." I collapse into her and she hugs me. Both of us are crying now.

Eventually I sit up and wipe at my eyes. "So," I say, laughing weakly. "How have you been?"

She smiles and nods a little. Her hair is long; I've been keeping mine short. "I'm all right," she says, and I can feel the truth of it. She has a calmness that I've always dreamed about. I think about the butterfly and the tornado. I read a book about it once — it's called sensitive dependence on initial conditions. Her eyes are contented. "Mostly."

"Still having those nightmares?"

"Yeah. You?"

I nod, and let out a breath. "You married?" I ask. She nods. "Kids?"

She shakes her head. "We thought about adopting."

I give a chuckle. "There are plenty of kids out there who could use a good home." I stare at my hands. "What's his name?"

"Kevin."

"Good guy?"

She nods. "Kinda boring, but.. you know."

I nod. "Boring can be better than the alternative."

She sighs, and a moment passes. "Did he.. you.. a lot?"

I close my eyes and it all comes back. I'm seeing red. Over and over. By the end it was once a week, at least. "Over and over," I say.

"You can't just keep running," she says.

I push my hands into my eyes and water escapes. "I know," I say quietly.

After a few minutes she stands up. "I'm turning you in," she says.

I look up. "What?" I ask and jump to my feet. "How could you—"

She pulls out a pair of scissors and grabs her hair and slices. She pulls the clumps away and throws them in the river. "Gimme the green hoodie," she says.

I hesitate. "Laura, you can't.."

She takes off her black coat. It's wool, soft. She holds it toward me. "It's the only way I can get you to forgive me."

I shake my head, slowly. "I forgive you," I say. "I'm not letting you do this."

Her arm sags a little, still holding out the big warm coat. "Well, then.." She pauses and looks into my eyes. "It's the only way I can forgive myself."

I think about it, then nod a little. I unzip the green hoodie and hand it to her and take her coat and put it on. It smells of lavender. I put my hands into the pockets and feel a ring of keys and a wallet.

She zips up the hoodie and smiles at me. "My car's up there," she says, gesturing to the embankment above us. "There's some money in the wallet."

"Laura—"

She smiles. "Call me Maria. I need to get in the habit."

I laugh, then stop and look up at her. "It's not your fault," I say.

She nods. "Yeah, I know. But.. you know. 1999."

I shake my head. "I'm not going to lie. I've been angry."

"And maybe your anger made you—"

"Stop it."

"Yeah, okay."

Then I hug her. The lavender mixes with the funky smell of the green hoodie and my tears and snot. "I'm not letting go," I say.

She reaches into her jeans and pulls out a small grey plastic thing. "This is an audio recorder," she says, and pulls the cap off. "And a flash drive." She hands it to me, along with a handwritten note. "Talk into it and mail it to Sebastian, along with that note."

I read the note and smile. "It's from mom."

She nods. "Yeah, the agoraphobic." She takes a breath. "He'll put it in the mailbox and you can get it."

She smiles and I realize I'm looking at myself. We hug again.

I step back and sigh. "Be careful," I say.

She nods and pulls the coat closed. "You too."

I turn and walk up to the road. I put my hands in the pockets of the hoodie and play with the cap on the flash drive.

I check into a cheap hotel. I write "Maria Gonzales" on the card and it feels weird.

Later that night I stare at the phone. Finally, I pick it up and dial.

Kevin answers in a tense but weary voice.

"Hey," I say, just louder than a whisper.

"Oh my God," he says. "Where—"

"I can't talk long," I say. "I'm going to be gone for a while."

"Laura, what—"

"Shhh. I told you, I don't have much time." I can see the red and blue lights outside. "You have to find someone else."

"Laura, there is no way anyone else—"

"I'm sorry I can't tell you more." I push a hand to my face, holding back the tears. I hear footsteps in the hallway. "I love you."

"Laura, tell me what—"

I hesitate and mutter "I gotta go" and hang up the phone. A second later the door splinters and explodes and two cops storm into the tiny hotel room, guns drawn.

April 2012

"You're *twins?*" Sebastian stared at her. Laura smiled a little and nodded, drinking her coffee. The cafe was empty, but music was playing and they felt safe talking.

"She's two minutes older," she said.

"Why didn't she tell me?" he asked.

"She was protecting you," Laura said. "So was I. You're an accomplice."

He scowled into his coffee. "Does your mother even live in that apartment?"

She shook her head. "We never knew our mother." He looked up. "She abandoned us and we grew up in foster homes."

"Here?"

She nodded. "Here and there. Most of them sucked."

He gazed out the window. "Sorry." he said.

"Not your fault." She drank. "Anyway, when we got older we made up a story about how our mom lived in an apartment but was scared to come out. That way we could pretend to be normal but we had an excuse if anyone wanted to meet her."

"Fooled me," he said.

She sighed. "In 1999 I did something really horrible. We had a fight and we split up and we never spoke again."

"And then she went away, and you sent me the flash drive."

She nodded. "I knew she trusted you, so we made you the bag man."

"Why not just visit her?"

She paused, for several minutes. "I can't." She looked at him. "I wish I could tell you why. No one deserves to know more than you." She put her cup down and reached out and grabbed his hand. "You've become the most important person in her life, Sebastian." He smiled a little. "I mean it," she said. "You have no idea what your friendship means to her." She took the cup again and drank. "And to me."

"I hate dealing with secrets," he said, scowling into his coffee.

She nodded. "I know," she said. "Me too." She sighed. "Believe me, I held that secret about '99 for eleven years. Tore me up every damn day." She looked up at him. "We'll tell you eventually, I promise."

He nodded. "I know." He drank. "I guess you had your reasons before, so I'll trust you for now." He sat back. "But it had better be one hell of a story."

She smiled. "Rest assured, it's one of the best stories you'll ever hear." She sighed. "In the meantime, please keep visiting her."

"Of course. And you?"

She pulled the flash drive out from her pocket. "I only came here for this."

"She said it was 'the last one'."

Laura nodded. "Yeah, we're all finished with it now."

"Where will you go?" he asked.

"Chicago," she said. "My husband misses me."

"What's his name?"

"Kevin."

"He treat you right?"

She nodded, with a little smile.

"You treat him right?"

She chuckled. "I try."

He grew serious. "Don't keep secrets from him."

She sighed. "Just one," she said. "Just until she gets out."

He nodded slowly. "I guess you know what you're doing."

"I hope so." She drained her coffee cup and placed a ten-dollar bill on the table. "I need you to do one more thing with me."

"Sure," he said, standing up. They left the cafe and went into a nearby alleyway. She produced the flash drive and kissed it. Then she put it on the ground and picked up a rock. She handed it to Sebastian. "You sure?" he asked. "You don't want to keep it for, like, a memento?"

She shook her head. "It's time for this thing to die."

He nodded and crouched down and brought the rock down on the grey plastic thing three times. Shards of circuitry and plastic flipped around. He stood up.

She hugged him. "Thank you, Sebastian."

"You're welcome," he said.

"I'll see you in January 2022."

He nodded. They walked out to the street and she hailed a cab and it drove away.

2012

I am in my cell. It sucks, prison sucks. I try to kill time with cards and basketball. I've got a pretty good poker face, but I'm terrible at basketball. I'm about to go to sleep when an alarm starts ringing. I hear some shouting and the word "fire" sounds in the distance. Guards go running off. I go to the bars but of course I can see nothing.

When I turn around, my sister is in the cell with me.

"How did you get here?" I ask.

She smiles. "I have my ways," she says, and unzips the dark green hoodie. She sits down on the bed.

"Go away," I say. We are speaking in tense whispers, a steady rhythm that layers itself on the lowest levels of voice. We can hear each other over the ringing alarm, but just barely. "I told you how this is going to work."

She shakes her head. "I thought about it," she says. "A lot." She sighs. "It's not fair. Not fair to you, and not fair to me."

"I told you—"

"I know what you told me. And I told you how angry I was. I'm still angry." She looks up, her eyes damp. "But you don't deserve this."

I sit down beside her. "Neither do you."

"Maybe not." A moment passes. "But Kevin definitely doesn't."

I start crying. "He's gotten used to it," I say. I know she's right, but I resist.

"I called him today," she says. I look up with alarm. "I told him I'd be home soon."

"What did he say?"

"I didn't give him a chance to say anything." She takes my hand. "He sounded worried." My mind reels. Three decades of our lives whirl around and overwhelm me. I collapse into her. She strokes my hair. "Go back to him," she says. I nod weakly.

After a few minutes, I stand up and take off the uniform. She removes the green hoodie and her jeans and I realize, once again, that I am looking at myself.

We get dressed. She struggles a little as she zips up the jeans. "You've put on some weight," I say. She chuckles. "It's good," I say. "You look healthy."

We hug. "I love you," she says.

"I love you too."

"Parole in ten?" she asks. I nod, and she says "I'll see you then."

The alarm stops ringing. I turn to face the bars. "Go," I say.

And then I am alone.

May 2012

Laura opened the door and Kevin rose from the sofa and knocked over two empty bottles on the coffee table. The room's only light was the blue glow of the silent television. He stumbled over to her and grabbed her. He cried into her neck and she sighed. "I'm so sorry," she said.

"Oh God," he said. "What happened?" He pulled away and wiped his eyes. "Where were you?" She looked at him, her eyes heavy with sorrow. He scowled. "Please tell me what happened." She looked down and he turned quickly and went back to the sofa and sat down. She unzipped the green hoodie and hung it on a hook on the closet door, then sat beside him.

"I want to," she said. "I hate asking you for this."

He stood up. "You can't expect me to just accept this. Do you have any idea—"

"Yes," she said, standing. "I know what you went through." He started to talk, but she pointed at him. "I know you think I don't, but I do." She lowered her voice to a place next to silence. "I know what it's like to think that the person you love most in the world might be dead. I really do understand that. I know about the fear, I know about the pain."

He glared at her.

"I do," she said again. "I know that you cried yourself to sleep sometimes, and you wondered what sort of pain she might be in, if she's even alive. I know how you left a light on some nights, just so she could find you in case she somehow came back."

He nodded a little. "I did."

She tried to smile. It was hard, but she managed to. "Well," she said. "I came back."

He let out an angry breath. "I can't do this if you don't tell me."

She stepped to him and took his hand in hers. "Can you wait ten years?"

He tilted his head. "Why?"

She sighed. "January 2022," she said. "I'll tell you everything."

He hesitated, a long, frustrated moment of heat and fury and sadness. Then he exhaled and pulled her close. "I guess I don't have a choice," he said.

"Thank you," she said, looking up with a tearful smile. They kissed. "I love you," she said.

"I love you too." He hugged her again. "I'm just so glad you're home." They stood there for a moment, wrapped in the blue light. "Come on," he said, switching it off. "Let's go to bed."

And for the first time in her life, she slept through the night.

for Diane

Love cannot conquer all if it is not conscious.

Ewuare Osayande

The most intense love affair of my life began on a Wednesday.

I remember, because I met her at a meeting of the campus anti-sweatshop group, which met on Wednesdays. She was the best thing that ever happened to me. I'm still trying to figure out what I did to make her leave.

The Sweatshop Working Action Group was a tiny cluster of students who wanted to do something about the horrible stories we always heard from third-world countries where our clothing and cell phones and laptop computers come from. The group had some t-shirts made, with the acronym real big and the name of the group in small type. Most people didn't read the small type and rolled their eyes or made fun of me for wearing it, so I just stopped.

We met in a small classroom on the second floor of the political science building. Most of the people who came were ludicrous in their idealism, but it was something to do and it got me out of the house. It's easy to feel paralyzed by the enormity of everything, so I kept busy to drive that feeling away. She was the first one to show up at our first meeting of the year and I was second.

She was reading *War and Peace*. An apt title, considering everything that happened. I paused for a moment, outside the door, far back enough from the little window so she didn't notice me. She had on a mottled brown shirt that blended with her smooth copper skin, and a long dark *batik* skirt. A bicycle helmet sat propped against a grey-and-orange carrier bag beside her chair. She had one leg tucked under her, a hand gently held to her temple as she read. A few strands of her black hair hung thoughtfully in front of her face — enough to intrigue but too few to suggest apathy. The rest of her hair was restrained to keep it out of her way, but those strands announced the depth of her immersion into the book she was reading. They fascinated me in a way I could not fully appreciate, a synecdoche of her physical beauty's juxtaposition with intellectual intensity.

I came in and pretended to be surprised that someone else was already there. "Hey," I said, pulling off my backpack and sliding into a seat three spots away. The desks were arranged in a semicircle, facing a whiteboard on the north wall and a projector hanging from the ceiling.

"Hello," she said, and I froze with the enchantment of her accent. Indian British, just barely noticeable in those two simple syllables. My mind flooded with doubts and second-guesses in the four seconds before she spoke again. *She's obviously too beautiful to not have a boyfriend. You're scrawny and awkward so there's no way she'd be interested. She'll break your heart like Cristina did in high school. She's way out of your league. You've never even left the country. You're too white for someone gorgeously cosmopolitan like her. What makes you think you have anything in common?*

The absurdity of this last one was made obvious when she asked, "This is the anti-sweatshop group, yeah?"

I nodded. "Yeah." Again, my mind buzzed with the passionate implications of her words and elocution. The positivity and incidental foreignness of her last word murdered my composure. Or at least that's how it felt. *She knows why she's here and she obviously knows exactly what she wants and it's not you. And why should it be? Are you turning into one of those scummy dirtbags who goes to political meetings to pick up chicks? You can't be that lonely already. It's only been two months since you broke up with Jen.* Fortunately before I started wallowing in that nightmare again, my obnoxious extroversion kicked in and I scrambled out of the chair and stepped over to her and put my hand out. "I'm Mitch," I said.

"Oh," she said with a smile, and snatched her bookmark from the back of the book and dropped it in and shook my hand. It was all perfect fluidity, like she'd spent her childhood doing nothing but dropping bookmarks into place and closing novels. "Vandana." She had a blue wristband on, with recessed letters that I couldn't make out. It slid down her arm and brushed against my hand as she shook. Her grip was confident but gentle. If I wasn't actually in love with her by that point, the handshake is what did it. Not the trite hogwash about electricity when we touched — I had burnt those sensations out of my skin's imagination years ago — but (as with everything else) it was *how* she shook hands.

Not how she shook *my* hand: how she shook hands, period. When we first meet another person, regardless of the silly snap judgments clouding our minds, the handshake doesn't alter itself to betray some feeble emotion. We just shake hands like we've trained ourselves to do. If you always shake hands with aggressive power, that's how you'll shake the President's hand or the hand of your eight-year-old nephew. And once again, her handshake imprinted itself on me as reflective of her assertive ambiguous allure. An ephemeral five-fingered *je ne sais quoi*.

Some guys are intimidated by confident women; I've never understood that, and they won't admit it, so there's no point in asking. For me the confidence is part of the attraction — if she knows what she wants, how much more remarkable would it be if that thing she wants is *you*?

Then again, that's always a long shot, and it's mostly out of your hands. Maybe that's why so many guys look at it as a game. You can *win* a game, and you can quit playing and you can finesse the rules. Coming at it honestly makes you vulnerable and you tend to look weak. And (assuming you let it, which I always do) the little hater in your head will become your worst enemy. *Seriously*, he started asking, *what do you expect will happen here? One handshake and you lose your mind.*

I tried to tune him out. "What are you reading?" I asked as I sat back down.

She rotated the spine toward me. "Tolstoy," she said. "I read *Anna Karenina* for a course last year and loved it."

"How is it?" I asked. Her bookmark was halfway down the book.

She nodded. "It's good," she said, and brushed those strands behind her ear. They drooped slightly and threatened to escape again. "I only just feel like I'm getting to know the characters."

"He's Russian, right?"

"Yeah," she said. "Nineteenth century." She smiled. "I've been on a bit of a nineteenth century bender. I just got done with Zola."

I made a blank face, looked to my left, and shrugged a little.

"He was a French novelist," she explained. "Naturalist, all about coal miners and prostitutes and people getting crushed by money and society."

I smirked. "Sounds familiar."

She tilted her head slightly — almost imperceptibly. It wasn't coy or seductive but suspicious. Almost skeptical. If it had been more pronounced it would have been condescending. "Are you being crushed?"

I could spend forever dissecting the devastation I felt when she spoke, and I'm trying not to. But the slight upward tick of the last word in her question did something to me. Most Americans will ask such a thing with honest, if aggressive, banality. The British interrogative sometimes adds a gentle softening to the final word, a touch of authentic curiosity that conveys a glimmer of concern.

I shrugged. "A little."

I was saved from having to pull an explanation out of my ear by the arrival of two more people, one of them the lead organizer. True to anti-authoritarian form, the group disdained titles like "president", but the "lead organizer" did everything a president would do. His name was Darren, an energetic sophomore from upstate New York. We were the only two people who had shown up for the first meeting when he'd started the group in the spring. We attracted some new people over time; most of them drifted away. We kept at it, because we didn't know what else to do.

Darren loved to wear t-shirts with open button-down shirts over them. That day he wore his upside-down swoosh tee with a black dress shirt on top. He carried a cardboard box with files and rolled-up signs crammed in. A blonde woman with a tie-dye shirt was with him.

He smiled as he came in and set the box down on the table near the whiteboard. "Hey, Mitch," he said, and shook my hand. "How was your summer?"

I shrugged. "I've had worse jobs."

He nodded. "Cash rules everything around me."

"Gotta get paid."

"Oh, indeed." He grinned and turned a little to face the woman and Vandana and me. "This is my girlfriend, Kristen." I made a quick smile of congratulations to him as she waved at Vandana.

Kristen gave a smile that felt rehearsed and tired, and held her hand out to me. "Hey," she said.

"Hey," I said, "nice to meet you." Her handshake was timid and fleeting and I started thinking about Vandana's handshake again.

Two more students showed up and Darren started the meeting. It was interesting to meet the new people and learn about them. Kristen was a freshman who had no idea what she wanted to study and didn't know much about "political stuff". I talked about my journalism major and the time I went to a WTO protest. Then I listened with rapt fascination as Vandana described her exchange-student status and how she was involved back in Leeds with the anti-war movement and a feminist news collective. At one point Kristen said something about "I love your accent" and I was embarrassed — because it's a somewhat shallow thing to say, but also because I felt the same way and I was relieved that someone else was willing to say what I was thinking.

The instant we started onto actual business, however, it became — as usual — something of a chore. Regardless of the justice of the cause, or the charisma of the people involved, meetings are by their nature dull and tedious. I often wonder if the rank-and-file meetings of the Southern Christian Leadership Conference were boring too, despite the presence of Dr. King and Ella Baker.

The hour was made worse by my knowledge that it would soon be over and I would be lucky if I ever saw Vandana again. *You could try asking her out,* the little hater said, *but why bother? The odds can't be better than ten percent, and even if she said yes, you know something would go wrong.* I couldn't argue with that. *Something always does.*

I tried to tune him out. Darren suggested that we work on pushing a licensing code of conduct for the campus. I offered to do some research on codes adopted by other schools. Vandana volunteered to contact someone in the athletic administration office, which gave me a chill because it meant she'd be back next week. She glanced around. "Does anyone here do sport?"

It was another one of those moments when my heart froze and I hesitated inside the exquisite difference, all because of one dropped *s*. I smiled with a couple of others and we all shook our heads. *That's a minus point*, the little hater said. *She's obviously athletic; look at her bike helmet. Don't you think she wants someone who goes for a jog once in a while? What, you think because you ride with Critical Mass every other month you're kindred spirits? Get real, dummy.*

Sometimes after a meeting Darren and I would hang out, grab a bite. That wasn't going to happen with Kristen in the picture. When we finished, I decided to save myself the embarrassment and pretend like I had somewhere to be. I gave a little wave, said "Have a good week" to the room, and left. I made a quick detour into the men's room, enduring more abuse from the little hater all the while. I went down the side staircase and left through the east doors to decrease the chances of running into anyone, but I forgot about the big bike rack and when I stepped outside there she was, undoing the lock and she looked up and I suddenly noticed the blue TARDIS decal on the helmet she was now wearing and she smiled and those strands of hair were back in front of her face and I almost collapsed and started crying.

"So what are you being crushed by?" she asked, swinging her bike off the divider post with a fierce purpose matched only by the constant astonishing fluidity.

"I'm being crushed by your stunning beauty," I said. "Your graceful passion seeping through every action you take and every word you speak with that amazing Indian British accent is destroying the wall of icy detachment I've spent the last three months building."

Of course I didn't say any of this, nor was I capable of even developing such coherent thoughts. Instead I gave a chuckle that was meant to convey cool *ennui* mixed with the maturity that resists the urge to babble about one's problems to others — especially people you don't know very well — and said: "Oh, you know. The Man."

She nodded, but didn't let my words evaporate. "And which man is that?"

I turned my palms up slowly. "You know," I said again, and ordered myself to stop using that phrase forever. "*The Man*. Mr. Burns. Bill Gates. Sam Walton. George Bush." I looked around as we reached a busy intersection and I realized she was walking with me. She removed her helmet and fastened it to her shoulder bag. "Where are you headed?" I asked.

She gestured vaguely with her head, keeping her bike steady between us. "I'm staying at the co-op on Gilman."

I somehow managed to keep the chills from overwhelming me once I realized Gilman was in the other direction and she was walking with me for some other reason. The little hater was quiet while he tried to figure out how to adjust.

Autumn in Madison, Wisconsin is a blessed relief from the muggy summer. The lakes surrounding the isthmus fill the air with humidity and mosquitoes, both of which abate gradually when classes start in the fall. As we walked, the youthful exuberance of the new students bubbled on the sidewalks and streets. Revelers in the taverns and patio cafes welcomed the setting sun with good cheer, a relaxed counterpart to the intensity of school. I always felt glad to get away from the campus at the end of the year, and I was always glad to return in the autumn.

"I'm three blocks that way," I said, pointing up the street. Maybe I thought she'd peel away but fortunately she did not. "I usually bike around, but it's so close.."

She nodded. "I always find somewhere else I want to go, so it just makes sense to bring her along with me."

"Her?"

"Julia." She glanced at her bike. "Julia, meet Mitch."

I raised an eyebrow. "Uhh."

She bent down and did a high-pitched ventriloquism. "Nice to meet you."

I laughed and shook my head. "Wow," I said. "People call me weird."

"Oh, what?" she asked. "You Americans have no sense of humor."

We Americans? The little hater paused, and I paused with him. What did that mean? *It means she sees you as just another vulgar beer-guzzling idiot.* "What are you talking about?" I asked. "We're funny."

She waved a hand. "It's all curse words and shock humor," she said. "But when a bicycle talks you call it weird. You've probably never heard of Nina Conti."

She had me there. "It's just unusual," I said. "Usually it's just bells and brakes. I didn't realize they had the power of language."

She crouched and did the voice again. "Well it's time you learned the truth."

I laughed, even though I was still bristling at the "you Americans" thing. *See?* the little hater said. *She hates Americans. Give it up, pal.*

We walked for a few moments in silence. The sounds of traffic mixed with passing music and people outside relaxing.

I looked down and noticed her bracelet again. "What does your wristband say?" I asked.

She shook her arm to rotate it, and held it to my face. The words "We Stand With Malalai" were stamped in sans-serif letters. "Who's Malalai?"

She rolled her eyes a little. I felt myself get tense. *Sorry for not knowing who that is.* I couldn't tell if it was me or the little hater.

"Malalai Joya," she said. "She's an awesome woman in the government of Afghanistan." Two "on" sounds in that country's name did erotic things to my ears. "We had a campaign at uni last year and sold these."

I nodded. "That's cool. Was it a successful campaign?"

She shrugged. "Sort of. We made exactly as much money as we spent on the wristbands."

"That's annoying," I said. "Sounds like the sweatshop group."

"What d'you mean?"

I waved a hand. "We go out with tables, try to get people to sign petitions. Three hours gets you four signatures. It's pointless. No one really cares."

"It's not so bad," she said. "I bet you get more than that. Besides, those four people care." I shrugged. "Or maybe you're tabling at the wrong spot." She giggled. "You're not setting up outside the pub, are you?"

I smiled. *See?* the little hater shrieked. *She's one of these naive idiots who doesn't recognize what we're up against.* "It doesn't matter where you set up," I said. "No one's paying attention."

"Well," she said, "Americans aren't known for paying attention."

There it is again. The little hater was doing a victory dance. *If this is how she feels about Madison, imagine her reaction to Mississippi. Or Texas!*

I was suddenly in the odd position of trying to defend my country while despising its apathy. "I don't know," I said, leaning my head back in controlled exasperation. "Americans aren't bad, they're just distracted."

She smiled. "You're all so proud of how little you pay attention to the rest of the world."

I shrugged. "Yeah." *She's talking about Malalai*, the little hater said. *Wait 'til she finds out all the other stuff you don't know.*

"But that's not an excuse, is it?" She looked at me sideways. Again with the upward spike at the end. It stuck to me with a sensual grip. "You're in journalism, yeah? Well, what's that about, if you don't want to enlighten people?"

"It's just so much bigger than most people even realize." I kicked a rock on the sidewalk. "Even this license agreement thing," I said. "If we get it passed—"

"When we get it passed," she cut in.

"Whatever. What will it really do? The companies are already setting up whitewash committees, making it look like they're doing the right thing, and starry-eyed kids here feel better and then we all go play hacky sack."

She made a gesture of mock defeat. "So now you don't like hacky sack?"

"When you look at the big picture, what difference does it make?"

She let out an annoyed sigh. "When you look at the really big picture, we're flakes of dead skin on a rock spinning around a dying star and it all goes pear-shaped soon anyway, so who cares?"

"Yeah, exactly."

"But we're here. And we can fight back." We took a few more steps. "It matters," she said. "You must know it matters."

I shrugged. "Maybe."

After a few more steps, she climbed onto the bike and clipped her helmet in place. "I know what you need," she said.

"Oh yeah? What's that?"

"You need to have dinner with me on Friday night." She tilted her head a little with confrontational poise. She adjusted the strap on her bag and I looked at the logo of a camera lens with *Aperture Science* written underneath.

"And why do I *need* to have dinner with you on Friday night?"

"Well, because I have things to read tonight, and I have an essay I have to write tomorrow." She gestured obliquely. "But I like to have fun on the weekend, and I don't have any mates here yet. So let's get something to eat." She waited as I tried to figure out how to respond in a way that was neither clichéd nor obnoxious. "You're planning to eat dinner on Friday night, yeah?"

I nodded. "Yeah, I don't see why I wouldn't."

"You've not developed photosynthesis powers, have you?"

"Not that I know of." I flexed my fingers and looked at them.

"Great. Come to the International Co-op at seven?"

I smiled. "Sure."

"All right." She nodded at my shirt. "And you can explain what 'Yell Fire' means." I glanced down at the image of Michael Franti and when I looked up she was cutting across the street and racing away.

My favorite restaurant in Madison is a little Thai-Lao place called Vientiane Palace. The building has seen better days and it's in a weird spot with a tiny parking lot. But no one goes for the atmosphere. They go for the food.

When I showed up at the co-op she was reading on the front porch. She had on blue jeans and a black shirt with a stick-figure man running into a blue circle. The little hater was bombarding me with all the possibilities for disaster. *Don't blow it, dingus. What am I saying? Of course you will. You'll think you're being cute, but she won't bother to see beneath the surface and only the negativity will show through and she'll get annoyed and suddenly next week she'll have other things to do.* I swore I would keep things positive.

She glanced at her watch, then ducked inside to stash the book — revealing the back of her shirt, where the man was emerging from an orange circle — and emerged with helmet in place.

"Tell me about the crash," she said.

I scowled. "What crash?"

"The crash you were in where your helmet got shattered. I assume you haven't had time to get a new one. Or maybe you're betting the law of averages will protect you for a while."

I made a face and looked askew. "I'm a daredevil," I said. "I laugh at danger."

She put a hand over her mouth. "Maybe you can't afford one," she said. "Are you very poor? How insensitive of me." She unclicked her helmet and held it out. "Would you like to use mine?"

"No thanks," I said. "I'm good. The Man can't tell me what to put on my head."

She laughed and strapped it back on. "Yeah, take that, The Man! I reckon Bill Gates will start dismantling his corporate empire once he hears you've suffered a massive brain trauma from smashing into an SUV." She laughed as she spoke, beguiling in her mockery. It was still annoying, but I was keeping it positive.

"Pfff," I said. "Any SUV in my way needs to worry about how *I'm* going to damage *it*."

"Sorry," she said, carrying her bike down the porch steps, "does SUV stand for something different here? Because in the UK it's a huge two-ton machine that can crush a kitten's skull without noticing."

"Did you want to get dinner?" I said, aware that I was snapping a little. *Told you. What a great way to start a date*. Keep it positive. Gotta keep it positive. I told myself that she started it, but of course that didn't matter.

"Yeah," she said. "Where are we going?"

"Have you been to Vientiane Palace?"

She gestured. "That's right up the street here, yeah?"

I nodded. "Yeah."

"I ride by it all the time. I'm a bit scared to go inside."

"You don't have to be afraid," I said. "I'll protect you." I pushed off and we darted through cars and locked our bikes up and went inside.

A middle-aged woman of southeast Asian extraction scowled at us as we entered and held up two fingers. I nodded and she shoved a pair of laminated menus into my hand and gestured to the empty room of tables. We walked to the back and sat down at a wobbly table near the window.

"Service with a smile," Vandana said. I pushed the table against the wall to quiet the shakes and shrugged.

"I don't care who brings the food," I said. "Wait 'til you taste it."

"All right," she said, perusing the menu, "but I'm trusting you."

"I always get the same thing," I said. "Pad thai. And we should get the *tom yum* soup." We can get it with shrimp, or .. You're not a vegetarian, are you?"

"Most of the time, I am."

I grinned. "Oh thank god." I closed my menu and set it on the edge of the table. "I was worried we were going to have some weird discussion about eating meat."

She narrowed her eyes. "So you *don't* eat meat?"

I shook my head slowly. "Nope. Can't stand it."

"You don't get cravings?"

"Not really."

"God," she said. "I miss chicken so much."

"That's why you said 'most of the time'?"

"Yeah." She closed the menu. "I'm just so glad to be living in a time with good fake meat. I wouldn't have been a very good hippie vegetarian in the sixties. Just bean sprouts and turnips." She made a face.

The woman approached and dropped two glasses of ice water. She made a grunt that I had come to interpret as "What would you like to order?"

"Tom yum with tofu," I said. "And pad thai for me."

The woman scribbled without making eye contact. "How spicy?" she asked in a flat voice.

I paused. *She'll think you're a wuss if you say mild.* "Medium," I said. *Still wussy.* The woman scribbled some more.

Eventually Vandana decided it was her turn.

"I'd like the spicy plate," she said. "With tofu."

"How spicy?"

She glanced at the stars on the front of the menu. "Four stars," she said.

"Very hot," the woman said. "You want three stars?"

Vandana smiled. "My family is from India," she said. "Four stars, please."

The woman gave her a look and snatched up the menus. She turned to go.

"Oh," I said. "And a thai iced tea, please. With cream." I looked at Vandana. "You want one?"

"No, I'm fine with water," she said. The woman walked off.

"So," Vandana said. "Yell fire."

"Yeah," I said. "It's an album from this guy named Michael Franti." I drank some water. "I liked his earlier stuff better. He's gotten kinda touchy-feely lately."

She nodded. "What sort of music?"

"Sort of a global funk blend with some hip-hop. He used to be in a band called Disposable Heroes of Hiphoprisy. That had more hip-hop and industrial in it."

"I love hip-hop, me," she said. "I expect you've not heard of Braintax or Dubbledge?"

"Uhh," I said. "What?" I started feeling stupid again.

"They're British rappers. Lady Sovereign?"

I glanced around and shrugged a little.

She smiled. "We got an indie garage scene" — the pronunciation of *garage* was like silk — "with this grimy sound. Not like the bling-bitches crap over here."

"It's not all bad," I said, surprised that I had to defend American hip-hop. "It's just no one's heard of the rappers who are talking about real stuff."

She shrugged. "Maybe not," she said.

"Okay," I said, determined to stay positive. "Your turn."

"What?"

"Julia?"

She scowled and softened. "Oh, my bicycle." She nodded and drank water. "There's a comics writer named Julia Wertz, she did a book called *Drinking at the Movies*. She makes comics all the time about riding her bike, so I figure Julia's a good name for a bike."

The woman delivered the large dish of soup and plopped down two small bowls, then retreated to the counter and began preparing my tea. She returned and set it down with only a few drops sloshing over the edge. Vandana chuckled and I started ladling the soup out.

"Yeah," I said, quietly. I was horrified the woman would hear and become offended. "My guess is they know their food is so good, it doesn't matter how they treat their customers."

"What are you gonna do?" Vandana said, taking a bowl. "Go somewhere else?"

I laughed. "Some places they come by and ask how the food is. Not here."

She laughed too. "Hey," she snapped. "How's the food? It's good, isn't it?" She jabbed her spoon at me. "Yeah, we know. Shut up and eat." She ate some of the soup. "Oh wow. This *is* good."

I nodded. "Yup." We ate in silence for a moment.

She drank water. "Oh, this is spicy."

I ate. "It gets worse at the bottom of the bowl," I said. "Do you think you made a m—"

"No," she said, cutting me off. "I can handle it."

"There's no shame in asking for three stars," I said.

"Maybe not in *your* family."

I paused. "What, really?"

She grinned. "No, of course not."

"So," I said, finishing my bowl and retrieving a second. "What's Aperture Science?" She was chewing, so I gestured. "It was on your carrier bag."

She nodded and pointed to her shirt. "It's from a video game called *Portal*. You've never played it?"

Another thing you don't know, the little hater said. *What a dumb, ignorant American you are.* I shook my head. "Last video game I played was Tetris." *Why say that?* the little hater barked. *You could have pretended to be cool and said you play video games. You would have something in common. Something to talk about. Man, you suck at this.*

"You're joking," she said, helping herself to more soup. "What do you do all day then?"

I shrugged. "Read books, watch movies."

"All right," she said. "What movies?"

"Hang on," I said. "Tell me about this *Portal* game."

She hesitated, then leaned forward, eyes glimmering. "Right. So you're this woman named Chell, and you're trapped in this place called the Aperture Testing Facility. And there's a robot named GLaDOS trying to kill you." I nodded. She moved her hands with that devastating fluidity while she spoke. "And your only weapon, yeah, is this portal gun."

"What's a portal gun?"

"Right. So it shoots these portals, yeah? A blue one and an orange one. Let's say you put the blue one here," and she gestured to the wall beside her, "and the orange one on that wall." She pointed to the wall on the other side of the room. "Enter one and you come out the other."

"That's interesting," I said. "Or the ceiling?"

She nodded. "Wherever."

The lady brought our meals, with a bowl of rice, set them down, and walked off without a word. Vandana's plate was swimming in oily redness. She scooped some rice onto her plate and doused it with soy sauce, then shoveled some of her order on top. She made it through two forkfuls before she grabbed her ice water and guzzled, then said "gah" and seized my iced tea and gulped it down. I chuckled as she began chomping the ice.

She leaned forward, breathing heavily. "Oh my god," she said. "What have I done?" She looked sideways at the dish, onions and bamboo shoots rising jaggedly through a lake of pepper sauce.

I pushed my pad thai toward her and she helped herself, trying to dilute the bits already on her plate. She ate it slowly, her eyes watering and her breath moving in quick bursts. I ordered more water and another iced tea.

After dinner we dropped the leftovers at her co-op and rode up to the terrace on the lakefront. A mediocre band was playing, so we wandered along the shore to avoid the ruckus. "Do you want something to drink?" I asked, glancing toward the booths in the distance.

"No thanks," she said. "I don't think I'll be able to taste anything for a few days."

The last vestiges of sunlight were evaporating, and we found a quiet spot on the far side of the pier.

The little hater tried to intervene, but I was enjoying myself too much to notice. Much. *Enjoy it while it lasts, schmuck,* he said. *I give you a week at the most. You're already getting tired and it's only eight. What are you even going to talk about? You're not interesting enough to keep this going. Just give it up now and save yourself the trouble. You could go home and watch Futurama or something.*

She sat down, dangling her legs over the edge. Her shoe skimmed the water, sending little ripples outward. I watched them until they vanished into the darkness. "Okay," she said. "Movies."

"Yeah," I said. "I've watched a few movies in my time. Like *Star Wars*. I saw that one." I leaned back with a pompous pose. "I'm pretty smart when it comes to movies."

"All right," she said. "Top five movies."

"Ooh," I said, sitting up. "Okay. *Blue Velvet* is up there, because David Lynch is just the man."

"I thought you said The Man was crushing you."

"Not The Man, like The Man, but .. you know, he's the *man*."

"You're not making a lick of sense."

"Whatever. *Spinal Tap* has to be on the list."

She gestured to her shirt and altered her accent a bit. "This is my exact skeletal structure."

I shivered in a rush of eternity as the stunning ecstasy of the moment washed over me. Without prompting she was spitting dialogue at me. I recovered and said "But it's not green."

She pointed with those elegant fingers and smiled. "It *is* green," she said. I leaped on her and kissed her, with passion and relief. It was euphoric and blissful and amazing.

Of course I didn't. But I did nod and grin and I looked at her for a little too long because she looked at me too, but then she looked away and said — a little too loudly — "Number three."

I gazed into the water. "Yeah. Uh, I saw this new movie last month called *Primer*. It's really weird and really confusing, but it's really good."

"What's it about?"

I paused. "I'm not really sure," I said. "There's these two guys and they make a box or something, and then it lets them go back in time."

She made a face mixing intrigue and skepticism.

"But they can only go back to when they start the machine up. So, like, six hours or whatever."

"Sounds odd."

"It is. It's really weird."

"I like time travel stories. Have you read *The Time Traveler's Wife*?"

"No," I said. "But this is the best time travel movie I've ever seen. You should definitely see it. Maybe you can tell me what's going on."

She shrugged. "Do you have it on DVD? You doing anything tomorrow?"

"Yeah, I'm watching *Primer*."

"You should come to the co-op in the afternoon. Some of my housemates will watch it too."

The little hater started in again. *She doesn't want to be alone with you. She wants to have an out if you start getting weird. She probably won't like it, and her housemates won't like it either, and you'll look stupid. Why don't you pick a different movie?*

"Yeah," I said. "All right."

"All right then," she said. "Four."

"Four o'clock? Sure."

She chuckled. "Four o'clock is fine, but I meant number four on your list."

I stared into the water. It was no good to impulsively list the first titles that came to mind. I needed to show off the range of my experience and tastes. Science fiction was covered. David Lynch was covered. Comedy was covered. Maybe an action movie?

"Did you ever see *Shadowlands*?" I asked. She shook her head. "It's about C. S. Lewis and how he fell in love with this American woman. It's really good, but it's sad."

"So long as it's sad for a good reason."

"Yeah, it is. I loved the Narnia books when I was a kid, so I expected it to be more fantasy, but it's still really good."

She nodded slowly. "I only read the first one," she said. "I got caught up in *Lord of the Rings* and it seemed like Narnia couldn't compete."

"Yeah, *Lord of the Rings* is great. Did you like the movies?"

"Of course. Didn't you?"

"Yeah," I said, and paused.

"What?" She sounded disappointed.

Keep it positive. "Nothing," I said. "There was just so much hype. They were good."

"Okay," she said, moving us thankfully along. "Number five."

"Robocop," I said.

She leaned forward and gave me an incredulous look. "The robot policeman?" she asked. "The action movie?"

"It's really good," I said. "It's violent and gross and silly, but it's got some really important stuff in it."

"The cop who's a robot? We're talking about the same film here, yeah?"

"Shut up," I said, hoping I was pulling off the playful tone. *Yeah, good*, the little hater quipped. *Tell her to shut up. That'll get her to like you.* "Have you ever seen it?"

She laughed. "I'm afraid not."

"Well, don't judge it until you see it."

She kept laughing, and sensed my tension, so she made herself stop. *You're getting all bent out of shape about a movie. Don't forget about the helmet argument earlier. You're really sweeping her off her feet, Romeo.*

"Okay," I said, smiling to force myself to drop it. "Let's hear your top five."

"Blast," she said. "I knew you were going to ask that." She pulled her legs underneath her and counted off on her fingers. "*Snatch* is up there," she said. "I like *Lock, Stock* too, but I feel like he didn't really get the pacing right until *Snatch*."

I felt stupid again because I had no idea what either of those movies were, but I pretended like I'd seen them both and that I knew who "he" referred to.

61

"*Rang de Basanti* is one of my favorites," she said, and smiled at me. "Don't feel bad. No one in this country has seen it."

"Is it Bollywood?" I asked.

"New Delhi," she said. "Bollywood is just what comes out of Mumbai, but there's lots of other movies made around India."

Another bit of your ignorance you've revealed, the little hater said. I shrugged. "Ya learn something new every day." I nodded. "So what's it about?"

She let out a breath. "A lot of things," she said. "These five guys get hired by a British woman who wants to make a movie about her grandfather's war diary, and then all these things go wrong and they start to look at everything differently."

"Sounds interesting."

"Yeah," she said. "The cross-cultural elements are really well done."

"That's two," I said.

"*The Matrix*," she said. A conventional choice, but there's no denying it's a great movie. "Trinity's such a bad arse," she said, and I smiled at the adorable word.

"There is no spoon," I said.

"Absolutely," she said. "I actually dressed up like Trin' for a costume party once."

"Oh yeah? With the leather and everything?"

"Pleather," she said. "No need to kill a cow to look cool. But I glued some washers onto my arms — you know, like the plugs for the input jacks — and it left this nasty rash for weeks." She rubbed her forearm and peered at it. "Can't really see it anymore."

"Too bad the other two movies sucked."

"Actually," she said, and I stood up with comedic hyperbole.

"Say one more word and I'm going home."

She reached up and pulled on my hand. It was the first time we really touched after the handshake and it was all warm softness with silk beauty wrapped around my palm. I sank more with the collapse of infatuation than the force of her arm.

"There's a commentary track from these two philosophers," she said. "You ought to listen to it. I didn't like the second and third movies too much either, until I heard the commentary. It really makes a lot of sense. There's a lot of things I didn't realize."

I looked sideways. "I dunno," I said. "All that fighting in the third movie. It got so boring."

She nodded, her head tilted a little. "Yeah, of course. They're not perfect. But I appreciate them a lot more now than I did before."

"Okay, so anyway," I said. "What's number three?"

"I dunno," she said. "Monty Python should be on the list."

"Can't call yourself British if it's not."

"It's a bit problematic for me to call myself British anyway," she said. "But we'll say *Life of Brian*. I really don't get Christianity, so it sort of stands out."

"Why is it problematic to call yourself British?"

"Well," she said, "I'm not sure if you know this, but Britain and India have a bit of a rocky history. You see—"

"All right, all right," I said, feeling as stupid as she made me sound. "I didn't know if there was some other reason." *You're such a moron*, the little hater added. *Would you ask a black person in America why she wasn't celebrating the Fourth of July?*

"Some other reason than hundreds of thousands of people getting killed and decades of—"

"Hey," I said, snapping again. So much for keeping it positive. "I'm sorry." I scowled into the water. "It was a stupid question." *Three arguments on your first date. This is one for the record books.*

"It's okay," she said. "I *am* British." She looked at me softly, her eyes gentle in the evening light. "It's just.. complicated." She paused. "No worries."

"Okay," I said. "One more."

"*Crouching Tiger, Hidden Dragon*," she said.

"Yeah," I said. "I saw that. With the flying kung-fu and all the special effects."

She nodded. "But like with *The Matrix*, it's got a lot of philosophy too."

"I don't really remember any of that. I remember people tip-toe-ing along tree branches."

"Yes, but there's so much about Buddhism and mercy and teaching."

I shrugged. "Maybe I need to watch it again."

She smiled. "My housemate's got it on DVD," she said. "Maybe after we finish *Primer* tomorrow.." She rolled her eyes with a little shrug and I smiled back.

There was a loud groan when the credits rolled.

"Are you having a laugh?" Vandana asked. Her housemates Daba and Mateusz shot me angry looks.

"Is there a problem with the DVD?" Mateusz asked. "I think it skipped some things at the end."

I chuckled. "I know, it's crazy."

"So what is going on?" Daba asked. "How can you like this?" He gestured to the TV.

"Hang on," I said. "Keep an open mind. Let me just tell you what I think is going on."

"Talk quickly," Vandana said, crossing her arms and dropping back onto the couch. I was on a recliner to her right. Daba was beside her and Mateusz had pulled over a chair from the dining room.

"Okay," I said. "There's an A end and a B end." I chuckled again. "No, actually, I don't really understand that part. But they're going back in time, okay? They turn the machine on at eight AM" — I put my right hand out to one side — "and then they go to Russellfield, to the hotel."

"They take themselves out of the equation," Daba said.

"Yeah," I said. "They don't want to change anything."

"But the guy brings his cell phone," Vandana said.

"Yeah," I said again. "He does. We'll get to that." I let out a breath, trying to organize my thoughts. *You sound like a moron*, the little hater said. I managed to ignore him. "Okay, so at the end of the day, they figure out which stock did the best that day." I put my left hand out to the other side. "And then they go back to eight o'clock." I moved my left hand to meet my right.

"And then they buy a lot of that stock when they're back in the morning," Mateusz said. His glower was softening.

"Right," I said with a grin. "So they're just making money at first. And it works pretty well."

"Until the guy brings his cell phone," Vandana said. She was still scowling.

"Yeah," I said. "Sort of. But they said they both felt fine. So the problem didn't happen until later."

Daba was tapping a finger to his temple. "He said they broke symmetry."

I pointed at him. "Yeah, exactly. So somehow that led to Thomas Granger finding out."

Vandana scowled more. "Who?"

"Their last and best hope of funding," I said.

She let her frown go. "Oh," she said. "Yeah. He's somebody's dad, right?"

I nodded. "Yeah, the girl who's going out with the blonde guy."

"Granger is the comatose man?" Mateusz asked.

"Yeah," I said. "In the guest bedroom." That line won me a couple of smiles.

"So what does this have to do with the guy at the party?" Daba asked. "With the shotgun?"

"Yeah," Vandana said. "I didn't get that part at all."

"I don't really know," I said. "I'm still trying to figure that out. But it has something to do with Aaron drugging himself."

"With the milk," she said, nodding slightly.

"Yeah," I said.

"Which one's Aaron?" Mateusz asked.

"The one with the dark hair," Daba said.

"Yeah," I said. "So he goes back in time and drugs his double, and then puts them in the attic."

"He does?" Daba asked.

"Yeah," I said, and paused for effect. "'Babe,'" I said, quoting my favorite line. "'They're birds. You don't want a bunch of dead baby birds up there, do you?'"

"Oh my god!" Vandana said, jumping up a little and pulling her legs onto the sofa. "That's him in the attic!" She put her hands in front of her mouth. Daba and Mateusz had slower, less exciting moments of awareness.

"Ohh," Daba said.

I grinned. "Yeah, I know, right? And there's lots of other stuff like that."

Vandana smiled. "Oh, I like that," she said, and grabbed the remote. "Let's watch it again," she said, pushing buttons.

"Are you insane?" Daba asked.

"Joking," she said, and turned the TV off. She looked at me sideways, with a tiny smile of grateful contemplation. A smile that said "I'm impressed".

"So what's going on at the end?" Mateusz asked.

I scratched my head. "Yeah, I'm not really sure," I said. "I think he's building another one. At some point he says something about making a box the size of a room, so that's probably what he's doing there. But I don't really know why."

"And what about the party?" Daba asked again. "And the shotgun?"

"I wish I knew," I said. "I feel like I understand more than I did the last time I saw it, but there's still a lot of stuff I don't get."

"Well," Vandana said. "It's quite unusual."

"But good," I said. "Isn't it interesting?" I glanced around at everyone.

Daba nodded, slightly. "I do want to see it again," he said. "I will probably understand more the second time."

"Definitely," I said.

"I don't know if I liked it," Vandana said. "We should definitely watch it again." She paused and smiled. "I want to think about it some more."

Mateusz stood up. "I have to go to the library," he said. "Thank you for the movie."

Daba rose as well. "Yes," he said, nodding to me. "I should do some work. Thank you." We watched him go upstairs. Mateusz put on his shoes, strapped on his bike helmet, put on his backpack, and left through the back door.

We were alone again. The little hater reappeared. *Time for you to screw this all up*, he said. *You think she's going to kiss you, don't you? As if! You're going to say something stupid and then think about it too much and then get angry at yourself but she'll think you're angry at her—*

"So," I said, as much to shut him up as to figure out the next phase of the evening. The sun was still up, but I could tell it would set soon. "Are you hungry?"

"Not really," she said. "I had a late lunch."

"Yeah," I said, looking around. "Me neither." The silence was awkward. "Do you want to watch *Crouching Tiger*?"

She shook her head. Her legs were still drawn up under her, but she was relaxed now. She was wearing a long dark blue skirt with a navy t-shirt. Her hair was down, little ringlets cascading off her shoulders. "No," she said. "I need some time away from movies now."

"Yeah," I said. "It kinda messes with your head."

She nodded. "In a good way."

I grinned. "You should see *Twin Peaks*," I said. "It's kinda like this, but .. less concrete."

She laughed. "*Less* concrete?"

I put a hand up. "All right," I said. "Maybe that's not the best way to say it. But it just feels like .. with *Primer*, I feel like most of the stuff I don't get, someday I probably will. But with *Twin Peaks* it's different. There's so much that's just plain weird."

"So what's that about then?"

"Well first of all it's a TV show," I said. "Each episode is like an hour long."

"How many episodes?"

"Thirty in all," I said. "The first episode is movie-length, so, like an hour and a half."

"That's quite a commitment," she said. *Hey look*, the little hater said. *That's a double-meaning there. She's not interested in anything long-term with you.*

"Yeah," I said. "But it's like nothing you've ever seen before."

"How so?"

"It just is," I said. "It'll change your life."

Another of their housemates came downstairs. An older woman with long curly brown hair. She smiled at us and went into the kitchen.

Vandana turned her attention back to me and smiled. "How did it change your life, then?" Her stress on the final syllable shattered me again. She wasn't asking with snark or attitude; she genuinely wanted to know. And I genuinely wanted to tell her. But I couldn't.

I sighed. "I can't explain 'it," I said. "You've just gotta see it." She shrugged. "Just let me show you the pilot," I said. "If you don't like it, I won't make you watch the whole series."

"What, now?"

I chuckled. "Well, no. But someday."

"Someday," she said with a slight nod. "Perhaps." *Yeah,* the little hater said. *You know what 'perhaps' means. It means never. It means shut up and quit pushing it. She's not interested.*

"They made a book, too," I said. "The diary of the woman who dies at the start of the show."

"A dead woman's diary?" she said. "That's intriguing."

"Yeah, it's good," I said. "Not the best thing ever written, but if you know the show it's got a lot of cool connections."

"Like *Frankenstein*," she said. "That's like the diary of a dead man."

"You know, I never actually read it," I said. *Yeah,* the little hater said. *Keep talking about what you don't know.*

She sat up. "Oh, you must do." Another flood inside as the phrase rippled through me. "Everyone thinks it's like the movie, where the monster just starts killing people for no reason. But it's not. There's plenty of reasons."

"You read a lot of classics," I said, trying to make it a question. *You sound like some whining frat boy*, the little hater said.

"I suppose," she said. "But it's not planned or anything. I just get into something, and .. go where it takes me." She paused. "What about you?" she asked. "What's the last book you read?"

"I read a lot of non-fiction," I said, shifting my weight in the chair. I wasn't uncomfortable, but we had been sitting for a while. "The last book I read was by this economist called *Bad Samaritans*. Chang something."

"What about?"

"About world trade. The subtitle is something like 'The Secret History of Free Trade'. He goes into all this detail about how the economies of the US and other countries developed. How government was so involved, even though we only hear about the free market."

"Yeah," she said. "And it becomes the way of the world for every other country."

"Yeah, exactly," I said. "He points out how hypocritical it is for countries that developed one way to demand that other nations go down this fake independent path of cutting public spending and services."

"And forget the environment."

"Yeah, exactly," I said again. *It's Broken Record Man*, the little hater said. *Say it again.* "It's like I was saying — all these institutions we're up against. It's pointless. Like our little sweatshop group can have any effect."

"Oh stop," she said. "What's that quote? 'Never doubt that a small group of committed people can change the world. It's the only thing that ever has.' You must know it's true."

"I don't know," I said. *Yeah,* the little hater said. *Here we go. This will lead to smooth romance.* "Whoever said that was living in a different time. The institutions are so different now."

"And the institutions Gandhi faced weren't violent and oppressive?"

I sighed. "I know," I said. "But that was about independence. I'm not saying it's easier—"

"Good," she said. "You better not." A little smile.

"But it's different," I said, trying to match her light tone. "It's a straightforward goal, with a clear objective, and everyone shares the bond of wanting that thing."

She nodded. "All right," she said. "I see your point. But it's like you've got no hope for the future. Things change." I was silent. "They change all the time. How did the Vietnam War end?"

I nodded just a tiny bit. "Yeah," I said finally. "But even that.." I trailed off, unsure of how to say what I didn't even find solid in my own head. "I mean, hope.." I sighed. "I like how Cornel West puts it." I looked at her. "You ever heard of him?"

She narrowed her eyes. "I don't know," she said. "His name sounds familiar for some reason."

"I read a thing from him one time about 'blood-stained hope'. About how you can't give in to some stupid sunshine optimism that everything's just going to work itself out."

"Yeah, all right," she said. "But it's still hope, isn't it?"

"Yeah," I said sadly. "I know. There's just so much that's wrong."

"I know what you need," she said, standing up.

"Oh yeah?" I asked. "What's that?"

"You need to give *Portal* a try." She moved to the stairs. "And I need to figure out where I know where I know this West bloke from."

I rose and followed her. *Into her bedroom,* the little hater said. *I'm impressed. Of course it doesn't mean anything. You're letting your hormones rush into something that doesn't exist. You'll find a way to screw this up, and you'll fall asleep alone, at home.*

Her room was spartan but tasteful. A mattress on the floor, mismatched light sheets layered on it. The hardwood floor featured a small square maroon rug. Books everywhere, including an overpacked case of shelves. On top was a statue of the elephant god whose name I can never remember.

She went to her desk, a tiny wire-frame thing with a laptop on it. She sat down in the chair, small and cushioned. I couldn't imagine working at a desk without a rolling office chair. She opened her computer and clicked the mouse, then typed with speed and grace. I was captivated once again by the fluidity of her movement, the flowing elegance of her fingers.

"Why do you use a mouse with your laptop?" I asked.

She shot me a confused look. "For games," she said.

"Oh," I said, browsing her shelves. Zola, Tolstoy, Dostoevsky. Rumi, Gibran. *The Bhagavad Gita, What the Buddha Taught, The Tao Te Ching.* bell hooks, Emma Goldman, Jane Goodall. Marge Piercy, Stanislaw Lem, Milan Kundera.

"Oh," she said suddenly. "He was in the second and third *Matrix* movies."

"Yeah," I said. "He has a tiny little part. I got so happy when I saw him on the screen."

She snapped her fingers, loudly. "That's where I know him," she said.

I scowled. "He's only on screen for like a minute," I said.

"No," she said, turning with a smile. "Those commentaries I told you about. He's one of the philosophers who does them."

"Really?" I asked, moving toward the screen. She had highlighted a sentence in the middle of the page: *In addition, West provides philosophical commentary on all three Matrix films in The Ultimate Matrix Collection, along with integral theorist Ken Wilber.* "Huh," I said. "Well now I really do need to check those out."

"Yes indeed," she said, and closed the web browser. She clicked a few more times and stood up. An odd picture of a man with a red water spigot dial in the back of his head appeared, and a pair of long ominous tones sounded.

I glanced at the chair. "Now I have to play this *Portal* game, huh?"

She smiled and pointed into the chair. "Now I'm *letting* you play *Portal*."

"It's pointless," I said. Three weeks had passed. We were at my place, killing time before dinner. I was browsing the internet and she was reading. I was in the big beige chair and she was on the couch.

She slapped the magazine closed. "Stop saying that," she said. "You're constantly on about how pointless everything is."

I made a face without looking up. "No I'm not." *Yeah*, the little hater said. *Here we go. What took so long?* He had been more vocal than usual lately. The proverbial honeymoon was ending, and I tried not to accept it with the fatalistic resignation he inflicted on me.

"Yes you are," she said. "No matter what we talk about, it's 'pointless'. There's no way to make a difference unless you can fix everything. You're like Rambo. It's this American attitude that you've got to save the world by yourself—"

"Why's it gotta be about Americans?" I asked. I scowled at the screen. "Why did you come here if you hate Americans so much?" *All right*, the little hater said. *You finally said the word hate*.

She paused and glared at me. "I don't hate Americans," she said. "I just can't stand this individualism you all seem to have." She gestured at me. "You've clearly got it, and you're an American, yeah?"

I sighed and looked at the wall. "Remember what you said about how you feel conflicted about being British?" I asked. She waited. "Well that's how I feel about being an American."

"Whatever," she said. "I thought Americans were supposed to have this fighting spirit." She gestured at me. "With you it's all 'The Man is too powerful. The Man has everyone brainwashed.'" She waved a hand with each point made. "The main person being affected by The Man is *you*."

"Look," I said, clicking another link. "I'm just being realistic."

"No," she said. "You're being pessimistic. You assume everything is destined to fail, so why bother trying?"

Even when she was chastising me, I couldn't escape the seductive rush of her pronunciation. Not *uh-soom* but *ah-syewm*. For a second I prepared to end the discussion because the sounds were melting me again.

"Lots of things *are* destined to fail," I said, glancing up and then back at the screen. "And I don't like wasting my time."

"Me neither," she said, and stood up.

Ha ha, the little hater squealed. *Kiss her goodbye, buddy. No, she probably won't even let you do that.* I closed the computer and put it on the coffee table. "Don't go," I said. "I'm sorry. Hang on."

She set her jaw and stared at the wall. Slowly, she sat back down.

"I'm sorry," I said again. "What do you want me to say?"

She raised a hand, low but authoritative. "Don't do that," she said.

"What?" I spread my hands.

"Don't make this a game of Simon Says. I'm not talking about specific things you say. I'm talking about how you look at the world."

I let out a breath and tried to control my frustration. *Go ahead*, the little hater said. *Let it out. This is stupid.* "How do I look at the world?" I asked.

"You see it through this prism of negativity and cynicism," she said, gesturing with supine hands. "Of course it becomes a self-fulfilling prophecy."

I nearly threw up my hands with a groan, but caught myself and did a more measured action of some kind. "But look at what's out there," I said. "This stuff isn't new. Everyone knows about sweatshops and toxic polluters, but they just think it's no big deal and they can keep living in this little bubble of theirs—"

"But they *don't* know," she said, cutting me off.

"A lot of them do," I said, loudly. *Louder*, the little hater said. *Get furious. You can win this argument!* "And if they don't, it's not because they can't learn about it if they wanted to." I made a disgusted face. "So what's worse — people not knowing and choosing to be ignorant, or people knowing and choosing not to care?"

She sat back. "So how do *you* know? How did *you* start caring?"

I hesitated. It was a good question, one I hadn't considered before. "I don't know," I said. "I had this teacher in high school who was always talking about human rights and stuff. So I asked him what books to read, and he gave me some."

She gave a little smile and shook her head slightly. "And don't you think it's just possible that you might have that same impact on someone else? And won't that make a difference?"

"Yeah, but meanwhile there's a billion people being lulled to sleep by reality TV and commercials for BP."

"Yes. And?"

I froze. I couldn't think of anything to say.

"What have they go to do with you?" She waited. I was silent. "Why are you so preoccupied with fixing everything, instantly, all by yourself?"

"Because it's never enough," I said. "People are dying and—"

"You think I don't know about people dying?" she said, standing. She was louder and angrier than I'd ever seen before. "I *met* Rachel Corrie." My eyes were getting wet. "My best friend from school was with her in Rafah. He held her hand as she died." She started to cry, but her indignation overpowered the sadness. "But you know more about suffering and the strength of elite power than me, right?"

I was speechless again. She sat down.

"You can know everything there is to know about all the systemic malfunctions around us, but if you can't see how beautiful the struggle is, then what's the point?" She wiped her eyes clear. "That's a *truly* pointless condition. Being unable to appreciate where progress comes from."

I sighed. I wanted to say something, but nothing made sense. Talking felt pointless. *You're just going to give up?* the little hater asked. *It's not like that girl's death even changed anything.* The silence hung between us.

"I'm sorry," I said. "I just feel really overwhelmed sometimes."

She sighed. "I know you do," she said. "We all feel that way. But you deal with it—"

Now I was the one interrupting. "I deal with it like this because it's what works for me."

"How's it working right now?" It was almost a whisper, but it cut into my soul and sliced something open. "What?" she said, louder, sitting forward. "You feel trapped, yeah? You feel like you don't have any way to get through." She smiled a little. "But think about *Portal*. You said it was like everything fell away when you went through that portal for the first time. Yeah? So that's what you have to do here. You've got to find some way to re-align your thinking. To see it all differently."

"It's not that easy," I said. "There's no magical doors like that in the real world."

"It's not magic," she said. "It's just a matter of thinking differently. And you can do that. You just have to work at it." She picked up a Revolution Cycles squeeze water bottle from the coffee table and held it up. "This is water," she said.

This is nonsense, the little hater said. *She's trying to change you, dude.* I sighed. "What does that mean?" *Another thing you don't know.*

"It's from a speech by David Foster Wallace," she said. "You need to read it."

I grabbed the laptop and flipped it open and found it in four seconds and started reading. Or I wanted to. Instead I let out a weak breath. "Maybe this is just how I am," I said. "This is just me. Maybe I'm just a little more cynical than you. That's who I am."

"It's not who you are," she said. "Who's the you that's saying that?"

I scowled. "What?"

"You can't jump in the same river twice," she said.

I looked up slightly. "What does that mean?" *Now she's a voodoo mystic*, the little hater said. *She'll have you sacrificing chickens next.*

"It means we're all constantly changing. It means your identity is always changing. Every day, every year."

I shook my head a little. "I feel exactly like I did last year," I said.

She paused and tilted her head. "So meeting me hasn't affected you at all?"

My blood ran cold. *She's got you there*, the little hater said. *Moron.* "That's not what I mean," I said.

"What did you mean?"

I took a breath and let it out. "I don't know," I said. "But there's a part of me that's constant," I said. "There's a core person behind it all."

She shook her head slowly. "No there's not," she said. "That's the ego. It's trying to pretend like it's you."

This conversation, the little hater said, *is over*. I chewed on my lip, avoiding eye contact. *We're done here*, the little hater said. *You should just end it now.*

"It's just a voice in your head," she said. "We've all got one."

This bitch is out of her mind, the little hater said. *She doesn't know you. She doesn't know what happened with your father. She doesn't know why you are the way you are. Three weeks of movies and dinner dates and suddenly she's psychoanalyzing you? And you're still talking about this? You're dumber than I thought.*

"But," she said gently, "you can quiet it." She stood up and sat down on the floor, cross-legged. "Come over here," she said, facing away from me. "You need to meditate with me."

I shook my head. "I'm not going to meditate," I said. "I don't believe in that stuff."

She paused, still facing away. "*That stuff*," she said with acid in her words. A moment passed and she rose again. "Everything that's not already in your head is 'that stuff'." She glanced at the coffee table and picked up the magazine. She held it toward me and pointed at the title. "What's that, then?"

I scowled at her. "What?"

"What's the name of this magazine?"

"*Z Magazine*," I said.

She pointed suddenly. "See?" she said. "That's exactly what I mean. You say 'zee'. We say 'zed'." She dropped it back on the table. "It's not right or wrong. It's just different." She looked down, and rotated the magazine slightly. "And now it's an 'N', right? It's all those things at once. And you can see that. It doesn't stop being an 'N' when you see it as a 'zed'. Or a '*zee*'." She said it with mock emphasis and smiled.

"Why are you making fun of me?" I asked.

She threw a hand up. "I'm not making—" She stopped herself and let out a breath. "Okay," she said, picking up the magazine. "I'm going. I'll call you later."

"No," I said, standing up. *Let her go*, the little hater said. "I'm sorry. Don't go."

She looked around and found her shoes and slid them on. "You're sorry, you're sorry. You're always sorry." She looked at me, a painful mixture of tenderness and pity. "I can't be here right now," she said. "If you won't meditate with me, then I need to go somewhere else and meditate by myself." She walked over and hugged me. I hugged back, weakly. *This is for the best*, the little hater said.

"Mitch," she said, drawing back and looking at me again. "I like you." She moved away. "But I don't always like being around you." She grabbed her helmet from the shelf near the door and strapped it on. "'This is water'," she said. "David Foster Wallace. Find it and read it."

And then she left.

One week later we met at a cafe on State Street. It was busy but quiet. I remember she was wearing the same mottled brown shirt and *batik* skirt she'd worn when I first met her. She was at a small table in a back corner, with a chair on the other side. She was reading *War and Peace* again. She was composed and beautiful and I was trembling with anxiety.

The little hater was blasting away at a mile a minute. *This is the end*, he said. *She's leaving and it's all your fault. Way to be so set in your ways. Way to talk over her and get defensive all the time. Way to sulk and make her miserable. Just like you did with Jen. You're so boring and predictable. This has nothing to do with negativity — you know that, right? This is about how dull you are. How long did it take Jen to get sick of you? About as long as it took to get to know you. To really get to know you. To peel back the layers of charming up-front good humor. You can only keep your real self hidden for so long. Sooner or later your idiotic, abrasive identity will come out and it will drive everyone away. Just get used to being alone. It's not so bad. You don't have to worry about what you wear or when you have to fart. You don't have to constantly check the clock to make sure you're not late for dinner or whatever. You don't have to listen to stupid nonsense about meditation and water.*

As soon as I sat down, I froze because I realized that I had totally forgotten to read the water speech she told me about. She looked sad, and she could tell how uncomfortable I was.

"Mitch," she said. "I have to tell you this is it."

It's over, the little hater said. *She's done. What a relief. She doesn't deserve you. You screwed it up. You made—* I pushed past him and said: "What do you mean?"

She shrugged a little. "This is the last time I can do this. If we can't work something out here, right now, then it's just not going to work."

My heart dissolved into something slimy and dripped into my lungs. I couldn't breathe and I didn't want to anyway. The little hater was right. I closed my eyes as he filled my head with scorn and anger and derision and mockery and bile.

I don't remember anything else about that conversation, except that it didn't end well. I admitted that I hadn't read the water thing. I apologized a dozen times, and she got more irritated every time. I tried to promise that I would make some changes, but she said I had made that promise before and nothing had changed. She wanted to know what specifically would be different, and I had no answer. I tried to approach it from a different direction, but it didn't work. Nothing worked. I'm still trying to figure out what I did to make her leave.

Finally, she stood up and put the book in her shoulder bag. With sad eyes and gentle steps, she walked around the table and kissed me on the head. "Good bye, Mitch," she said, and walked away forever.

Three Days Later

Three days later I went down to the terrace on the lakefront and sat watching the birds. After a few minutes I realized Vandana was off in the distance, sitting on the grass, meditating.

Don't even think about it, the little hater said. *Do not go over there. She said goodbye. Nothing has changed and nothing will change. What could you possibly say to her?*

I walked over to her and stood at a short distance. Her eyes were open but locked on the water. I waited and nearly ran away. She drew a breath and let it out. She looked over, as if expecting me. "Hey," she said.

I felt pressure behind my eyes. "Hey," I said. "Can I sit down?"

She paused and looked back into the water. "Yeah," she said.

Do not sit down, the little hater said. I pushed past him again and crossed my legs and sat on the grass.

"I want to apologize again," I said. "But I'm not going to." She smiled at this. I paused. "I read 'This is water'."

She looked up, still smiling. "And?"

I nodded. "You're right," I said. "It's amazing."

She nodded too. "Yeah," she said, and pointed to the lake. "This is water."

I gave a sad laugh. "It sure is." More pressure behind the eyes. I swallowed it down. "I've never been as happy as I was when you were in my life," I said suddenly, before the little hater could persuade me not to say it. "I didn't realize how happy I had been until I had to experience the misery of losing you."

"Mitch—"

"Hang on," I said. "I know what I should have said three days ago. Please just let me say it now."

She let out a breath and nodded. She wasn't meeting my eyes, but I knew that wasn't necessarily a horrible thing.

85

"I thought I knew what misery was," I said. "But I had no idea. The last three days have been nothing but misery. Real misery. I can't sleep, and I don't know what to do with myself."

A moment passed. "I've been sad too," she said, and finally looked at me. "But my days have been less stressful."

I looked down. I couldn't think of what to say.

"That voice in my head," I said finally. *What are you doing?* the little hater said. *Shut up. Get up and walk away. Do you really think this is going to end well?* "You were right about that." She smiled, just a little bit. "And I think .." I hesitated. "I think I know where I can find some hope." She stopped smiling and our eyes met again. "You're giving me hope."

Her eyes were getting wet. "You can't build your hope on a single person," she said. "What will you do when that person is suddenly gone?" I let out a breath. *She's not doing this again*, the little hater said. "But," she said. "I'm happy to hear that. Maybe we can help each other find some hope."

The little hater went into overdrive. *She doesn't mean it she's tricking you it's a trap this will only last a week and then you'll be right back where you were this morning don't even bother you're too stubborn to make any real change just give up now give up give up*

I wiped at my eye and moved my legs into a position matching hers. "Can I try this with you?" I asked.

She hesitated, then flung herself at me and we hugged. For real. Finally it wasn't a dream or a momentary hallucination. It was the hug of deep ecstasy, rushing blood and yes hormones, but even better, contentment. I held her with relief and a stream of euphoria. Then we kissed and she smiled and let go and wiped at her own eyes.

After a second she turned back to the water and crossed her legs and straightened her back. "Like this," she said, and glanced at me. I did the same, and she moved her hands to face me. She put the right hand out, then put the left hand on top, and touched her thumbs. "Just touch the tips together," she said. I mimed her action and she nodded and placed her hands in her lap.

"Now," she said, "keep your eyes open but don't concentrate on anything specific." She drew a breath and let it out. I did the same. "Just be in the moment." Another breath.

"Now, silently, count each breath." She inhaled. "One." She held it for a moment, then slowly let it out. "Two." Again, inhaling. "Three." Exhaling. "Four." She began breathing without words. I did the same, letting the numbers become the only thing in my head.

Or at least that was the idea. The little hater wasn't letting it happen. He kept ranting about how pointless it was, how uncomfortable my legs were, how hungry I was, how stupid we looked, how there were probably some hot chicks sitting nearby making fun of me.

Her voice cut him off. "When you get to ten," she said, "just start over at one."

I did. My breathing slowed down and I felt everything slow down. Including — I was shocked to realize — the little hater.

He didn't stop, of course. He kept going with the criticism and the sour commentary. But after a few minutes, I could hear the volume drop. Just a little; only a tiny bit. But it was real. I could feel it working. He started explaining that it was just an illusion, and it wouldn't work the next time, and I was wasting my time.

I pushed past him and kept counting.

The bell on her cell phone rang with deep resonance three times. We bowed and stood up. I held an arm out as she made it to her feet.

"You all right?" I asked.

"Yeah," she said, a hand on her belly. "He didn't want to stop," she said with a smile. "He was in total *samadhi*."

I leaned down. "Sorry, buddy," I said. "It's lunch time." I kissed her stomach. We don't know for sure it's a boy, but she seems certain.

It's been seven years now. I moved back to Leeds with Vandana. She finished her doctorate and got a position at the university. I got a job with a local newsweekly. I'm happier than I've ever been. She sponsors the Amnesty International chapter on her campus and I go to the meetings when I can. Last month I went with her to a video game convention and met some of her friends from online. Good people. Next year we're going to visit Scotland, to see the places she went with her mom before she died.

The little hater isn't gone, but he's a lot quieter these days. For a few months I stopped meditating and I could feel him get louder. So now it's once a day whether I want to or not. He's not going to win. I will *not* let that happen. I still don't know what I did to make her leave that time in the cafe, but he had a lot to do with it, and I'm pretty sure I can stop it from happening again.

I thought I would be confined by marriage, but I love it. It's not always easy, but we both remember what's important, and we let everything else go. I also realized in the second year that I was making fun of her a lot. Not out of cruelty, but gentle pushing back on her contradictions. Still, it was irritating her and I understood that I was crossing the line. I didn't just stop — maybe I can't, or maybe it's fun because she laughs anyway, when the joke up front is funny, even if the sentiment behind it is annoying — but I'm trying to make fun of myself more than anyone else. It seems to be working.

Everyone talks about marriage like it's some horrible cage you get trapped in, because you can't stand being alone or you want kids or whatever. I can't imagine feeling that way. Maybe I'll change as time goes on, but after seven years it just feels better all the time. We give each other space when we need it, and we can challenge each other without being overbearing.

I grabbed two bottles from the refrigerator and handed her one. "This is water," I said.

She smiled. "It sure is." The microwave beeped and she pulled two steaming bowls from it. She jabbed a pair of chopsticks into one and handed it to me, then began dousing hers with hot sauce. Thai take-out from a little place across town. It's not as good as Vientiane Palace, but it's the best in Leeds.

I went into the main room and turned on the TV. She sat down beside me and put her bowl and water on the table.

I hesitated. "You're sure, now?" I asked. She rolled her eyes with a smile.

"Yes," she said. "Start it."

"Because once we begin, there's no turning back." She grabbed for the remote but I held it away. "Okay," I said. "Okay." I hit play and set it down.

I picked up my bowl and began eating. I closed my eyes and smiled as the first chords of the *Twin Peaks* theme began to play.

Respawn

for Annie

When the imagination sleeps, words are emptied of their meaning: a deaf population absent-mindedly registers the condemnation of a man. [...] There is no other solution but to speak out and show the obscenity hidden under the verbal cloak.

Albert Camus

This story has been cleansed to remove profanity, naughty words, and ▮▮▮▮▮▮.

Three.

Two.

He pushed the left stick in.

One.

He was sprinting before anyone else moved. He hit Y and flipped his submachine gun around and pulled in the glock and tactical knife. He flew down the alley of the *favela* and chucked a stun grenade toward the corner. He began cooking the semtex even before the little x flashed, and when it did, he threw again. 100 for first blood, little window with his *Third Time Charm* triple-prestige title for all to see. *Mack928x3 shouldn't run with scissors*, he thought. Plus the truck was on fire. He waited a second, shot it twice, and felt the blast as it exploded and took another enemy combatant down. Another hundred. He switched back to the submachine gun and squatted. Holographic up, moving slowly. *Let him come to me*, he thought. He saw movement, but he didn't have a shot. Too far away. Two seconds. Three. *This guy has patience. Maybe it's Mack928x3 again, waiting because he knows where I am*. He went prone and slithered up behind the railing. Waited a second, ready to spring up. Then he heard fire to his right and saw the red dot in the mini-map. He got to his feet and spun around and raced into the little sniper house. Mack928x3 shot from the other direction and missed. *How did that other guy get to the sniper house so fast?* he wondered, then decided: *He must have taken the rooftops*. He dashed into the sniper house and wasted the guy and squatted in the corner and threw up the UAV and let out the breath he'd been holding.

The red dots were far away now, so he took a second to think. He switched back to the glock and knife and reloaded the glock. Then he pushed the left stick again and sprinted back to the smoldering truck. He ducked down and kept along the wall, then flew down the ramp and turned the corner and stabbed the guy hiding in the dark

95

spot. Mack928x3 again. *Man, he's gotta be pissed at me.* He spotted another guy dash into the garden-roof building, so he took off and caught up quickly and pushed the steel in and turned around again and barely caught the last pass of the UAV. They were all on the north side, so he ran back to the smoking truck and popped smoke for the sentry gun. The chopper came and dropped the crate and he grabbed it and saw all the green triangles on the west side so he ran east through the sniper house toward the barbershop.

Someone was waiting downstairs in the barbershop; he stepped aside just as the guy lunged out at him and then the guy fired his handgun wildly around but he was just a little faster and hit his target just in time and the guy dropped. Mack928x3 again. Third time's the charm. He ran upstairs and pulled out the sentry gun and put it in the sweet corner spot so it could see the street and the entranceway too and then he switched back to the submachine gun and went back downstairs and waited. He reloaded and waited as the sentry gun did its thing and just as it took down the ninth enemy Mack928x3 jumped around the corner and blasted him in the face until he was very very dead.

He smiled as he watched the killcam; Mack928x3 had crept like a wolverine, slow and steady, toward the barbershop. He knew where the sentry gun was and where his prey was hiding. And when he finally shot him he reloaded and emptied another clip into the corpse. *Can't say I blame him*, Germ thought.

Someone in his headset said "Dude that guy was pissed."

"Yeah," Germ replied. "Well, I got him three times in a row. I would be pissed at me too."

"They shot down your pave low too."

"Yeah I know."

"You suck at calling in choppers."

Germ made a face. "How can you suck at calling in choppers? That doesn't make any sense. You're an idiot."

"At least I don't ▮▮▮▮ suck at calling in choppers."

Germ rolled his eyes. "Shut up," he said.

Something moved in front of the screen and blocked his view. "Jeremy! Did you just tell me to shut up?" she asked.

"*You* shut the ▮▮▮ up," the voice in the headset said. "▮▮▮▮▮ fag. You're a little piece of ▮▮▮ with a ▮▮▮ the size of a ▮▮▮▮▮."

Germ closed his eyes and ground his teeth hard. "Mom," he said, "get out of the way!"

She reached back and turned off the TV. Suddenly he was back in his bedroom: grey chair, red-wine carpet, KMFDM poster on the wall over the TV. "Don't talk to me like that," she said. "You're lucky I didn't turn off the game." He sat back in his chair, pulled off the headset and let out an angry breath. She ignored this, stood glaring at him with her hands on her hips, a beige dishtowel clenched in the right. "I've been calling you for five minutes. Where's your brother?" she asked.

Germ held the guide button down for several seconds, then pressed up twice and hit A. "I don't know," he said, dropping the controller on the floor. "He said he was going out."

"Nice of him to tell me," she said and turned to leave the room. She moved back to the TV and turned it on again, but it was just blue. Germ got up and crossed the room to the bed.

"You can turn it off," he said. "I'm done." His mom clicked the set off again and closed the door as she left.

Two hours later, he was back in the same spot. Crouching in the barbershop, letting another sentry gun take down enemies. Another random idiot in his headset, whining about campers. *People camp because it works*, Germ thought. They accused him of camping all the time. Among other things. Lately it was care-package glitching. He stopped using them altogether, just to shut them up. *It's not me, it's them*, he thought. *I'm not doing anything wrong. But I'll change what I do anyway. As usual. The morons win again.*

Paul came online. Germ backed out and sent him an invite. He popped into the lobby.

"Germ man," Paul said. "What's up?"

"Nichts," he said. "What's up with you?"

"Nothin. Did you do the algebra stuff yet?"

"No. Just lemme see yours tomorrow."

"Whatever dude. Do your own ▉▉▉ homework."

"▉▉ you."

"Fag."

Germ set them looking for a hardcore headquarters game. He preferred team deathmatch, but Paul hated it. So they played HQ. It took three tries before they both made it into the game.

"God I'm sick of that," Paul said, once they were inside.

"Yeah, it sucks," Germ said, and glanced at the score. 2300 to 4700. "Jesus!" he cried. "Thanks for putting us on the suckiest team that ever sucked."

Paul laughed and said "Yeah, with these damn weiner kids." They could hear someone in the headset laugh. Germ hoped they got the *Simpsons* reference, but he doubted it.

The HQ location popped up and Germ sprinted for it. Glock and tactical, flying across the snowy base. He dipped behind a crate and waited. An enemy rushed past and he jumped out and stabbed him and moved into the HQ range. A few tense seconds and it came online. The bar filled at a crawl.

"Paul, where the ▇ are you?"

"Don't worry," Paul said. "I see ya. I see everything."

"Sniper dork."

"Better than being some gay running man."

"You could be here helping me capture."

In a half-second, Germ saw a bullet hit the wall next to him and he turned around just in time to see the guy drop.

"Yeah," Paul said. "But then I wouldn't be saving your ▇ when you're about to get shot."

With the bar half-full, a stun grenade went off and Germ pushed the stick left, trying to move but dragging himself like a drunk sloth. He cursed as the screen filled with light, and he saw his name pop up in the list of kills. He cursed again.

"Sorry dude," Paul said. "I tried."

"They're gonna capture it now."

"That guy isn't," Paul said.

"Is anyone on it?" Germ asked, more to the team than to Paul. As usual, no one answered. "Why the ▇ do you people have mics if you never use them?"

"I used my mic when I was ▇▇▇ your mom last night," someone said.

"I'm getting back into position," Paul said. "There's no one on it."

Germ sprinted back into the room and set up in the opposite corner. The bar began crawling again, and again a stun grenade went off. But this time he was ready, watched carefully as someone came ducking over the steps. Germ fired and dropped the guy. The bar crawled some more. A semtex started beeping, and went off just after he captured the HQ.

"I'm out," Germ said.

"Yeah, I saw," Paul said. "But you got it."

"No thanks to you." He clicked around until he found Paul's screen. He smiled and watched as the guy behind Paul waited just a second before stabbing him.

"Eat me. Oh ███!"

Enemies scurried around the HQ until it went away, and Germ pressed the left stick to start again. He knew they would lose, but he was determined to rank up before they did.

Friday night. Ashley was sprawled on his bed, texting Stephanie. Her dirty brown hair was splayed on his dark blue pillowcase, her hands moving furiously over the tiny keyboard. "The movie starts at seven-thirty," she said.

Germ sat hunched forward in his grey chair, peering into the screen. "I know," he said, running his harrier crosshairs over the map. He tried to predict where they were headed; the northeast corner looked like a safe bet. "But these invaders.. must die!" He said these last words in time with the music coming from the huge speakers on either side of the TV. A ripple of tiny *x*'s crackled on the screen, and he grinned as several yellow hundreds followed. He waited for two more to send him over the top for the pave low, but the strike ended. He spotted an enemy soldier in the distance and fired twice but missed. Then the guy dropped and he noticed Paul got the kill.

"Paul, you ███!" Germ cried. "You took my kill! I ███ hate you!"

Ashley sat up. "See?" she said. "There it is again!"

"Yeah, yeah," Germ said.

"Yeah what?" Paul asked.

Germ sighed. "Ashley's got this thing where guys always say they hate each other. She says—" Ashley yanked the headset off his ears and put it on her own.

"You *do*," she said. "You guys always go 'I hate you' when you're hanging out. And you're always punching each other and putting each other in headlocks. It's ▮▮▮▮ weird." She waited and listened. "Whatever. I think you say 'I hate you' when you really mean 'I love you, man'." She waited again. Germ shot a guy. "Whatever," she repeated. "We don't have time to discuss it. Now would you kindly finish this dumb game so we can go to the movie?"

"A slave obeys," Germ said.

Ashley froze, then slowly pulled the headset off. "Okay, that was too ▮▮▮▮ weird for words."

"What?" Germ took the headset back and replaced it on his head.

Ashley stepped back toward the bed. "You both said the same exact thing." She returned to the bed, back to the cellphone. "Come on," she said after a second. "We're gonna miss the previews."

"Hang on," Germ said. He crept toward the corner and waited, moved slowly, crouched for better aim. The red dot was up, edging around the side of the building; its chipped brick was blurry and he tried to ignore the flaming garbage can to his right. His left finger was clamped down, holding the sight up, his right finger poised tensely over the trigger. He took a breath, waited. "Just let me finish this round," he said.

Suddenly a guy flung himself around the corner and Germ sprang up and started firing wildly and so did the enemy guy and they both shot at each others' feet and into the walls and the guy backed up but he ran out of ammo first and just as he was about to reload Germ put the red dot in place and set up a headshot. Then everything went still. The round was over; they lost. "No way!" Germ shouted, punching his armrest. "I was just about to get my ▮▮▮▮ pave low!"

"That's because you're too gay for a pave low," Paul said in the headset. "Icy, doesn't that movie start soon?"

"Shut up," Germ said. "We're going."

"I'll be here," Paul said.

Germ stood up, peeled off the headset, and clenched his hands a few times. He turned off the console and his TV. Ashley was in front of the mirror, paused with her green hairbrush in her left, poised overhead while texting with her right. "Wow," he said. "I thought I was bad."

Ashley smiled. "Shut up," she said. "I just need to tell her something."

Germ rushed to her side to peer at the tiny screen. He spied several words before she shoved him aside and hit *send*. "Hey!" he said. "That game's not stupid! Show some respect!"

"Looks stupid to me," she said, stuffing the phone in her jeans pocket. "Come on, we're going to miss the previews." She took his hand and tried to pull him close, but he resisted.

He put a hand to her hair and smiled. "I wish you'd let me cut this."

She tried again, moving in to kiss him, but he moved upward at the last second and kissed her forehead instead. She froze, glaring at him. He smiled slightly and rubbed her palm with his thumb. She waited.

"What?" he asked.

She pulled her hand away. "You tell me."

"It's nothing," he said. "Don't worry about it."

She gave an exasperated grunt and turned to the door. "You get so tense when you play that ▬. I'm sick of it."

He chuckled. "It's not that," he said. "I just.." He shrugged at her back, watched her hair jostle as she shook her head slightly. A desperately thick silence dragged itself between them. He could see how jagged her eyebrows were in the reflection of the dormant TV. He wished he could call in a real-life care package, to get some new words that would make her not angry. But he needed an emergency airdrop, or maybe an AC130.

For Paul, he would need an EMP.

"Come on," she said finally, hustling toward the stairs. "We're gonna miss the previews."

Three hours later Germ was back in the lobby. He sent Paul an invite, and a second later he appeared with their buddy Mike.

"Hey Paul. Hey Mike."

"What's up," Mike said.

"Hey dude," Paul said. "How was it?"

"It sucked," Germ said. "I don't care what you say about Megan Fox, that movie was ▇▇▇ stupid."

"Oh my God," Mike said. "Dude, you're so right. He *is* queer."

"Shut the ▇▇ up," Germ said, trying not to get mad. "Maybe I just want some ▇▇▇ plot and character development when I pay eight bucks to see a movie."

Paul laughed. "In other words, you're as gay as Big Gay Al and Bruno put together, dancing at the Springfield steel mill."

"I guess you didn't ▇▇ Ashley yet, either?" Mike asked.

"You morons ready to play some deathmatch?" Germ said.

"Hang on," Paul said. "I need to change my title so it matches your purse." There was a pause. Germ flipped to the music player and started up The Crystal Method.

"You guys ever play that *Nitrous Oxide* game on the PSOne?" he asked. "That game was ▇▇▇▇ sweet."

"Nah," Mike said. "What was it?"

"It was this bug game where you were going down a hole and shooting at all the bugs. ▇▇▇▇ intense."

"Shooting bugs?" Mike asked. "Like in *Donkey Kong 3*? That's so gay."

"Dude, it was awesome. You shoulda played it."

"Okay," Paul said finally. "Check it out." Germ moved over to Paul's name and saw the light blue *My Little Pwny* title with the flower emblem. Mike laughed hard.

"That's cute," Germ said. "You ready to play?"

"Do hardcore," Mike said. "I can't take that softcore ▇."

"No way dude," Germ said, firing up Team Deathmatch Express. "I need to win some rounds tonight."

They were dropped in a team that was yelling full-tilt. Rednecks and black guys, each threatening to mutilate the other. Germ sighed.

"You ▇ ▇ ▇ ▇, I'd like to ▇ ▇ ▇ all over the ▇ ghetto."

"Come find me, ▇. I'm in Saint Louis, ▇ eastside. Anytime, ▇."

Despite their violent animosity, the Klansmen and the Black Panthers were beating the snot out of the enemy. Germ chuckled at the irony as he lit up a sniper with his submachine gun. He ran up the stairs and swung around to find another sniper watching the bridge. He stabbed the guy and turned around just in time to see a third enemy jump down from the sniping room. Germ nailed a headshot and sent up the UAV.

In the headset, meanwhile, the black guys had gone silent and the rednecks were trying to rile them back up. Germ imagined they had put the white guys on mute, which would be a smart move. But of course, people online usually didn't make smart moves.

Thirty seconds later, Germ was sweating in the dark room with the barrels, waiting for the guy near the big gas tank to show his face again. He only had seven bullets left in the submachine gun, and he doubted it would reach that far anyway. He thought about making a run for it, but he suspected the guy had a buddy watching from on top of the stairs. A flashbang went off across the way and Germ raced out. He dipped to the right and doubled back, spied the enemy in the distance and let loose. The seventh shot hit the guy's head and Germ finally got to call in his pave low.

He sat back and grinned as the beautiful green icon appeared in the mini-map. He didn't even mind when someone stabbed him in the back. He just nodded as his name appeared in the top right, showing off his *Third Time Charm* title. He panicked and left the room and went into the callsign menu and was about to change it, then he stopped.

He remembered a line from *Office Space*, and said it into the headset, even though he was alone now in the lobby. "Why should I change? He's the one who sucks."

Saturday night. They were in Paul's basement, playing splitscreen Special Ops. Paul was in his big blue chair, focused intently on the big plasma screen bolted to the wall. Germ was on the couch, much less centered. A bottle of ▆▆▆▆ Germ had swiped from his brother's closet sat between them, mostly empty. Germ was sliding onto his side, but Paul was barely buzzed. He sighed as Germ went down again.

"For ▆▆▆▆ sake," he said, racing to revive him for the fifth time. "Can't you stay alive for two minutes?"

Germ just laughed and started singing the Bee Gees, then switched to Homer Simpson. "Ah, ah, ah, ah, table five. Table five." He tried to stab a soldier in front of him, missed by a country mile, and got shot again. Paul threw the controller down.

"▆▆▆▆ ▆▆▆▆," he said. "This is ▆▆▆▆ pointless."

"Yeah," Germ said, dropping his controller. "I'm not really in any shape to kill terrorists right now." He looked at Paul, running his hands angrily through his hair. "You're not even buzzed, dude."

Paul held up the blue bottle. "That's because this stuff tastes like ▇." He took a pull and made a hideous face. "Why don't you steal something decent like ▇ or ▇?"

"Because Ryan doesn't keep that ▇ in his closet. Just me."

Paul jerked his head at him. "Just *what*?"

Germ reached out and grabbed the bottle. "Just this," he said, and took a swig. He looked at Paul, who still glared at him with confused fury. "Why? What did I say?"

"You said just you."

Germ laughed and offered the bottle to Paul, who shook his head slowly. Germ drained it and put it on the coffee table, and started singing a line from *South Park*. "Tom Cruise is in the closet..."

Paul shook his head but laughed a little. "Dude, if you got something to say, just say it."

Germ laughed and tried to keep his eyes open. He was slumped toward Paul. "Hey man, I'm gay. I'm a ▇ queer."

"Yeah," Paul said, flipping the TV to ESPN. "I know."

"Do you think—" and then Germ gagged as a thick clump of vomit spewed into his teeth. He put his hands up just in time to smear it on his chin and shirt. He bolted into the bathroom and heaved into the toilet; only half of the mess made it inside. He groaned and took a breath and then another wave hit and he spewed into the bowl again, wheezing in pain as the smell doubled back on itself and then throwing up some more.

Paul cackled with laughter at the disgusting sounds, and turned the volume up to hear the highlights of the Dallas-New York game.

From the bathroom, Germ coughed and spat. "Oh ▓, man," he moaned. "I'm so ▓ wasted." He looked down at the streams of saliva and semi-digested burrito on his shirt. He grabbed the towel beside him and wiped at the putrid mess. "Dude, I need to—" but he slumped forward and something cracked on a hard surface and he went silent.

Paul ran to the bathroom and froze. "Oh ▓ dude!" he said, and knelt down to Germ's bleeding head. He picked him up a bit and leaned him on the wall. Germ was conscious and laughed a little at himself. Paul rinsed the towel in the sink and wiped up the puddles of blood from the floor. "You're lucky you're my buddy," Paul said with a grimace. "This is some nasty ▓." He handed the towel to Germ.

"Yeah, I know," Germ said, and took the towel. He wiped his face clean, and pulled off the filthy shirt. "Do you have something I can wear?"

"Yeah, here." Paul grabbed a Florida State University shirt from a drawer and tossed it to him. It landed on the floor outside the bathroom.

Germ sighed and glanced at it. "Dude, I just threw up all over myself, but I have *some* dignity."

Paul smiled. "▓ Gator boy. Gay-tors. You do know that, right? That they're all gay?" He grabbed a red tank top and chucked it in Germ's direction, then sat back in the big blue chair.

Germ took a deep breath and wiped his chin one last time, then pulled on the fresh shirt. He took some toilet paper and did his best to clean up the area around the commode. Then he stood up slowly, balled the nasty towel, and threw it in a laundry basket in the corner. He stumbled toward the couch and collapsed on it, one arm over his eyes. "Dallas win?" he asked.

"Yeah," Paul said. "Overtime field goal." He sat with one foot on the seat of the chair, watching the replays.

"Nice." He took a deep breath. "Can I crash here?"

"Yeah, sure," Paul said. "Just don't puke on the couch or nothin'."

Germ chuckled. "I won't," he said. There was a pause. "But I *am* wasted." Another pause. A commercial for *Girls Gone Wild* rang in Germ's throbbing ears.

"Yeah," Paul said. Another pause.

"Dude," Germ said after a minute. "I'm serious."

As the commercial ended and a beer ad came on, Paul flipped through several channels. "Yeah, I know," he said. "You're totally ▮▮▮ up."

Germ waited. "No," he said. "Not about that."

Paul hesitated, then muted the TV. "What the ▮▮▮ are you talking about?" Germ tried without luck to figure out what sort of voice he was using.

"Remember what you said the other day about why I didn't like that movie?"

Paul turned his head slightly. "Germ, what the ▮▮▮ are you telling me?" He waited a second, then another. Then he stood up. Germ pulled his arm away and peered at Paul through the light from the halogen lamp.

Then he dropped his eyes and nodded a little.

"Oh my god," Paul said quietly. "Oh my god." He looked around helplessly. "You're.. You're.." He gestured with the remote. "You're wearing my ▮▮▮▮▮▮ shirt."

Germ sat up and steadied himself, unable to be as precise as he wanted. "What does that mean?"

"I dunno," Paul said, his face twisted slightly. "I mean, why are you ▮▮▮▮▮▮ telling me this ▮▮▮?"

Germ's face twisted too. "I dunno," he said. "I mean it's—"

"How the ▮▮▮ can you be gay, you ▮▮▮▮▮▮ idiot? You've got a ▮▮▮▮▮▮ girlfriend." He gave a quick shallow laugh and then pointed at Germ. "So that's why you haven't..."

Germ stood up and held a hand out. "Hey," he said. "Leave Ashley out of this."

"She doesn't even know, does she?" His face fought between smiling and scorn. "Gimme my shirt back."

Germ squinted at him. "What? Why?"

"I don't want you getting AIDS on it." He reached for the shirt but Germ slapped his hand away. "Hey!" He held his arms out, ready to respond.

"What the ▇!?" Germ cried. "One second you're my buddy, helping me clean up my puke, and the next you're calling me a diseased ▇ ▇ ▇!"

Paul threw the remote on the couch and shoved Germ toward the door. "Get the ▇ out."

Germ spread his hands. "What the ▇ is wrong with you? How have I changed in the last ten minutes?"

"You're not staying here tonight. Probably try to ▇ me while I'm asleep. Brokeback ▇."

"Are you listening to yourself? I'm not ▇ attracted to you. What is your ▇ problem?"

Paul pointed. "You make me ▇ sick. You're a goddamned ▇."

Germ dropped his shoulders and let out a quick breath. Then he lunged at Paul and clocked him in the face, dropping him to the floor. Germ stood over him. "Who the ▇ do you think I am? Who had your back when those kids were trying to steal your ▇ jacket? Did you forget that ▇? I wasn't such a ▇ then, right?" Paul scowled with acidic fury at him. "And what about when your ▇ parents split?" He waited. "Huh?" More waiting. "Who let you sleep over for a ▇ *week*? Who didn't tell anyone when you cried for twenty minutes that first night?"

Paul looked away, still scowling.

Germ spat on the floor. "▇ it," he said, grabbing his jacket from the shelf next to the TV. "You're an ▇." He pulled his jacket on and turned away.

"You've always been an ████████." He walked up the steps and slammed the door behind him.

A week later Germ was sitting in the dark on the floor of his bedroom. The blinds were closed; the only light was the green ring of his console and the screen of his cell phone.

"Seriously," Ashley said. "Why don't you come over or something? We can watch *The Princess Bride*."

"No thanks," he said. "I'm just gonna go to sleep."

There was a pause. "When are you gonna tell your mom?"

He gave a desperate chuckle. "In ten years," he said. "Maybe never." He let out a breath. "Man, Ash, you don't know how much I appreciate—"

"Stop it, Jeremy," she said. "You don't have to keep thanking me." She waited. "And you don't have to keep wallowing in your.." She adjusted her voice. "..*pit.. of despair*."

Germ tried not to laugh. Then he laughed. "Stop clapping before y'all make me smile."

"Okay, Shabazz K. Morton."

"Ash, I might have killed myself if it wasn't for you."

She paused. "You better be ████████ kidding."

He sighed. There was a silence. Then he yawned. "I need to sleep," he said.

"Call me tomorrow," she said.

"I will."

"Good night."

"Night."

He hit *end* and went to the TV. He turned his controller on and started searching for a game of Mercenary Team Deathmatch. Halfway into the game he saw Paul come online. He went to the user preferences and turned off notifications, then went back to the game.

Three days later he was playing Domination in the dark. No music, no headset. He realized halfway through the match that he didn't care if they won or lost.

Mike sent him an invite. He sighed and hesitated. Then he muttered "What the ▮▮▮▮" and joined the game. He plugged his headset in and waited to connect. Mike and Paul were waiting with three of their buddies.

"What's up guys?" Germ asked.

"Hey Germ," one of the other guys said. Someone from Paul's work. Germ didn't know him very well. "Where you been, dude?"

Germ paused. "Busy," he said. "Just.. doing stuff. We gonna play or what?"

"Yeah," Mike said. "Hardcore headquarters all right?"

"Hang on," Paul's work buddy said. "Lemme switch my classes."

"Make it quick," Paul said.

Germ flipped to the music player and started his Ministry playlist. "Stigmata" came on and he smiled.

"Okay," the guy said. "Ready."

Mike launched the game and after two false starts they dropped into a lobby with an annoying kid singing into the mic and two guys who sounded drunk. Germ's mind scratched at the noises in his headset, wondering if Paul was going to say anything.

The game started, and their team grabbed an early lead. Germ was in top form, his tactical knife slicing through enemies like a fork through soup. He captured the first headquarters and nearly shot Mike when he popped around the corner.

"Hey!" Mike said, startled. "Take it easy, dude. It's just me."

"Sorry," Germ said. "Hard to tell in hardcore,"

"Guys," Paul said. "There's someone on the other side of that wall."

Germ moved to the left and suddenly shots burst around him and he tried to figure out where it was and then the guy was dead and then Germ was down too.

"Oh ▮▮▮," Paul said. "Did I shoot you, Germ?"

He chewed his lip a little. "Yeah," he said.

"▮▮▮. Well, at least I got that other guy first."

"Yeah," Germ said again.

There was a pause. The music sent profanities around the room. "Germ," Paul said, then hesitated. "Sorry, man."

Germ smiled. He felt a wave of relief wash over him. "It's okay, dude." He went back to the fight.

They won two rounds and sat in the lobby waiting for the third to start. Germ took a breath. "I'm done, guys," he said. "I need some sleep."

"All right dude," Mike said.

"Take it easy, Germ," Paul's work buddy said.

"Yeah, I gotta go too," Paul said. "I gotta get up early."

"▮▮▮▮," Mike said. "Go get your beauty sleep, you queers."

Germ chuckled and backed out. He was about to shut the system down when he got a party invite from Paul. He tilted his head a bit, then accepted it.

Paul was the only one in the party.

"Hey," he said.

Germ let out a breath. He tapped the controller with his thumb. "Hey."

"I'm sorry," Paul said.

"I know. You already said that."

"No, I mean—"

"I know what you mean."

There was a silence. It was relaxed, filled with solace and comfort.

"Thanks," Germ said.

"Yeah," Paul said, then changed his tone. "Now. Would you kindly give me my shirt back?"

Germ laughed. "No, but I'll beat you to death with a golf club if you want."

Paul chuckled. "Hey dude, we should go bowling or something this weekend."

"Yeah," Germ said. "I get paid on Friday. Let's do it."

"Cool. Talk to you later."

"Night, man." He was about to unplug the headset.

"Hey Germ," Paul said.

"Yeah."

"I hate you, dude."

Germ smiled. "I hate you too, man."

The party went dead and Germ shut down his console and turned off the TV. The room became silent and he climbed into bed and fell asleep.

Kr Services, LLC

for Jim

No assassination instruction should ever be written or recorded. Ideally, only one person will be involved. [...] Assassinations can seldom be employed with a clear conscience. Persons who are morally squeamish should not attempt it.

CIA manual
c. 1954

Tyrone took a deep breath as he set the scope into position. Three hundred yards, he guessed. The guy was looking around. Nervous. Jittery. The flag dipped into view twice, and Tyrone flexed his finger over the trigger. The guy's uniform was stained. Probably ate too fast, or maybe he threw up before the fighting started. Tyrone waited one more second and fired the shot just as his cell phone rang.

He grabbed the phone and scowled at the number. 202 area code. Where was that? He pushed the green button and nestled the phone against his shoulder as he returned to the game.

"Hello."

"Hi, is this Tyrone Woodburn?" Some white guy, sounded around 40.

"Yeah." He saw another guy in the scope and started lining up a shot.

"Mr. Woodburn, my name is Earl Brinkman, from Kr Services. Have I caught you at a bad time?"

Tyrone rolled his eyes. "Sorry, man," he said. "Whatever you're selling, I don't want—"

"Actually, Mr. Woodburn," the man cut in, "I've got a job opportunity I'd like to discuss with you."

He hesitated. "What kind of job?"

"I understand you're planning to join the Marines after you graduate. Is that correct?"

He scowled again and quit out of the game. He hesitated. "How do you know what I'm planning to do when I graduate?"

"I'm afraid I can't go into the details over the phone. Why don't you come by our office after school tomorrow?"

"Why can't you just tell me?"

"Mr. Woodburn, this isn't an ordinary job offer, and it comes with some significant opportunities for advancement. I think it will interest you. Just come down and meet with me. If you decide—"

"Okay, hang on." He turned an envelope over and clicked a pen open. "Where's your office?"

Brinkman was tall and diesel, with a blue button-down shirt and a firm handshake. "Thanks for coming in," he said as he gestured to one of two chairs facing his desk. A big window looked out on downtown. They were high up.

Tyrone sat back, one hand on his knee. "Yeah, well, it's not every day some business guy calls me up with a job offer."

Brinkman smiled and pulled a file folder out of his desk. He put it down and leaned forward. "You play basketball, Mr. Woodburn."

He put a hand up. "What, 'cause I'm black? You assume—"

Brinkman sighed and opened the folder. "Two years at Farwell Middle School, one year at Kettering High." He looked up. "Right?"

Tyrone looked at the file but couldn't see much. "Why do you know so much about me?"

Brinkman tilted his head. "You know how colleges watch basketball players, to see who's got potential?"

"Yeah. Scouts."

Brinkman nodded. "Right. Well, they start pretty early."

"Yeah, like in middle school."

"Elementary, sometimes."

Tyrone spread his hands, then stopped. "This isn't about basketball, is it?"

Brinkman smiled. "No."

"But you've been.." He hesitated and scrunched up one eye. "Scouting? Me?"

He looked down at the file again. "Recently you took the Armed Services Vocational Aptitude Battery exam." He flipped a page. "Did pretty well."

Tyrone nodded and glanced around. "I did all right."

Brinkman flipped more pages in the file. "You ran track for two years. Doing well in your classes. No trouble with the law. You're smart .." He flipped another page and smiled at Tyrone. "But not too smart."

"When do you get to the part where you explain why you've been stalking me?"

Brinkman closed the file, folded his hands, and tilted his head. "This job opportunity brings with it a significant compensation package. Now, obviously we don't make this kind of offer to just anybody. We need to know some things about the people we approach."

"How long have you been doing this?"

"Quite a while," he said. "Fortunately, like most young people you're very generous with the details on social networking websites. And elsewhere."

Tyrone raised an eyebrow. "What do you mean, 'elsewhere'?"

"Before you took the ASVAB, you did some online test prep work. Do you remember that?"

He nodded.

"Well, one of the sample tests you took was from us. You provided a good deal of information there." He sat back. "And we've also been monitoring your online gaming skillset."

Tyrone scowled. "What?"

"Oh, sure. The military is using console controllers to fly drone aircraft. We watch reaction times, impulse control. There's lots of crossover there. Did you ever see a movie called *The Last Starfighter*?"

"No. Sorry, but.. What does your company do, Mr. Brinkman?"

He smiled. "We're a private defense contractor."

"What does that mean?"

"The US military has certain ways of doing things, certain rules it has to follow. When the government needs something done and doesn't have time for standard procedures, they come to us." He hesitated. "Think *Black Ops* but with a guy like me giving the orders, instead of the president."

"I dunno, man. The Marine recruiter said I could get money for college."

Brinkman smiled again and leaned forward. "Trust me, Mr. Woodburn. After one term of service with our company, you could pay for everyone in your family to attend the college of their choice."

Tyrone gazed out the window, then sideways at Brinkman. "So what would I be doing?"

Tyrone took a deep breath as he set the scope into position. Four hundred and fifty yards, no wind. Alpha squad was going in from the north, Omega from the west. They had the jump on this guy, no sweat.

He let out a breath and turned to his partner, a short guy named Ramirez. "ETA?" he asked.

Ramirez looked at his watch. "Three minutes," he said.

Tyrone nodded.

"How long you been in?" Ramirez asked. His voice was lower than Tyrone expected. Usually short guys had higher voices.

"Year and a half," Tyrone said, and glanced back to where Ramirez was gazing through his nocs. He shook his head a little. "Goddamned freshmen," he muttered.

"Hey," Ramirez said. "You started out green once."

"Pff," Tyrone said. "They didn't send me to goddamned Afghanistan for my first mission."

"Maybe you're not as good as me."

Tyrone gaped a bit, then chuckled despite himself. "Damn," he said.

Ramirez smiled without drawing down the nocs. "Uh oh," he said. "What the hell is that?"

Tyrone looked through his scope and found the target again. And the kid walking with him.

"I thought he was supposed to be alone."

"He was," Tyrone said. "This just got a little more complicated."

"Maybe now we can go for a capture instead."

"Shut the hell up with that," Tyrone said. "This isn't *Police Squad*. If he could be captured, why wouldn't they just send in the Marines?"

"I'm just sayin'."

Tyrone glared at him. "Well I'm sayin' you need to stop sayin'." He paused. "You feel me?"

"Yeah, fine. Whatever."

Two minutes later the Humvees dusted in and the guy pushed the kid to the ground and fired his AK. Tyrone took a shot and missed, but someone from Alpha took him out. They watched as one of the guys from Omega tossed an energy bar to the kid and pointed toward the village in the north. The kid hesitated for a minute and started running. The soldiers produced a tarpaulin, wrapped the corpse up, loaded it into one of the Humvees, climbed in, and took off.

Ramirez let out a breath. "Is that it?"

Tyrone stood up and brushed the sand away. "That's it," he said. "Let's go home."

"Oh my god," Ramirez shouted, running back to the table. "He told me I can get three of 'em for fifty bucks."

Tyrone rolled his eyes. The atmosphere called for a bit more discretion. They were dining in an elegant patio on a warm tropical evening. Everyone in civvies.

Everything was real wood: sturdy tables, comfortable chairs. Amazing food and rivers of beer. Soft light and good-looking wait staff. A perfect way to celebrate another successful mission.

"No way," one of the other guys said. Tall creepy dude with white hair. Everyone called him Anderson, but Tyrone suspected it was a nickname. "How long?"

"All night," Ramirez said, sitting down again. "This place is paradise."

Tyrone chuckled. "If this were paradise, why would we be here?" Laughs around the table.

"First time in Bali, huh?" Brinkman asked, eyeing Ramirez over a glass of *Henri Jayer Cros Parantoux*.

"Yes, sir," Ramirez said.

"Stop with the 'sir' nonsense," Brinkman said. "And have a good time." He drained his glass and stood up. "See you guys tomorrow."

The men stood and saluted. Anderson shouted: "K! R! What!"

The others barked back: "Silent! Deadly! Recognize!"

Brinkman clapped Tyrone on the shoulder. "Come here a minute," he said as he walked into the night.

Outside the restaurant, Brinkman lit a clove cigarette. "This is number forty," he said. "Right?"

Tyrone nodded back and glanced at the woman who held her hands open toward them. He wasn't used to ignoring beggars like the other guys were. "A little over two years," he said.

Brinkman flicked his ash toward the woman, just enough to scare her away. She retreated but didn't go far. "You're doing a hell of a job," he said. "Looks like we were right about you."

Tyrone nodded again. "I think so," he said.

Brinkman let out a line of smoke. "Three strays in two years is about average." Tyrone recoiled inside, but he'd gotten good at keeping his face blank. They weren't innocent civilians; Kr Services didn't even bother with *collateral damage*; they were *strays*. "How are the nightmares?'

Tyrone blinked away his wandering thoughts. "Not bad," he said. "The benzodiazepines are helping." They weren't, but there was no use in complaining.

"Good," Brinkman said. "Look, I can tell you guys have more planned for tonight, so I'll get right to it."

"Ramirez more than me," he cut in.

Brinkman smiled. "You taking estrogen shots, son?"

Tyrone threw up his hands. "Hey, I got plans, don't get me wrong. I'm just not following Ramirez to the herpes express."

"Tss," Brinkman said, dropping his cigarette and crushing it under his heel. "If that's the worst he comes out with, I'll start going to his church." He looked up. "We want you for something new."

"A special job?"

"More like a lot of special jobs. You ever hear of Wadjet Squad?" Tyrone shook his head. "That's right," Brinkman said. "That's because no one's ever heard of them, except the guys in it, and me, and three other people." He glared at Tyrone, deep. "But they're the reason you're still alive."

Tyrone scowled. "No disrespect," he said, "but I think that's because of my training and comrades."

"Yeah," Brinkman said, taking a breath, "you've been doing good work." He looked back at the table of guys. "And your comrades are strong. But without Wadjet Squad, the kids looking for revenge and the puppets of the masterminds would have taken you out months ago."

"I'm not sure I understand," Tyrone said. "But if this is what's next, I'm in."

Brinkman pointed at him. "And that's why. Right there. You're ready, you're able, and" — he softened into a smile and turned to go — "you don't ask questions."

Tyrone hesitated at the door. He could hear voices out on the roof.

"It was a kid," one of them said.

"It was a dog," another replied.

"It doesn't even matter," the first voice said. "The guy wasn't even 'Qaeda." His voice got more urgent. "Four weeks we were there and we saw nothing. No contact, no activity—"

Tyrone almost jumped when he heard a woman's voice cut in. "Hey," she said, cutting the first guy off. Footsteps. "For the last time. Shut the f—"

Tyrone threw the door open and shielded his eyes from the sun. The woman was standing inches away from a guy, her finger in his face. Four soldiers in standard Kr kit. M4s all around, two stun grenades each. The woman snapped her gaze at Tyrone. Her short dark hair flipped slightly.

"Woodburn," she said, and scowled at the other guy, who stepped back. "You're late."

Tyrone frowned and checked his watch. "No I'm not," he said. "You're all early."

She smiled, just a little. "In Wadjet Squad," she said, walking toward him, "you're early, or you're dead." She offered her hand. "I'm Phillips." She pointed to the other three, ending with the guy she had been chastising. "Jenkins, Delaney, Maxwell."

Tyrone nodded and looked nervously at Phillips. "I didn't realize—"

She pulled a knife from her belt and held it to Tyrone's throat. "Say it," she said, low and tense. "Say something about chromosomes." Eyes wide, Tyrone looked at the guys, who were making cautionary pantomimes of *Do not do that*. "Please," she said. "Say something about averages and dimorphism." He stared at her, and she stared back. "Please," she said again, pushing the blade in just a little. "I haven't killed anything in four days."

He waited and eventually she pulled the knife away. "Okay then," she said.

As she turned around, Tyrone whipped his rifle up and put it to her temple. "Don't ever do that again," he said.

She smiled and faced him. "There's only one reason I ever would," she said. "You don't say it, and I won't do it." There was a pause. "Deal?"

He glanced at the other guys, who watched, amused. He nodded and lowered his weapon. "Deal."

"All right then," she said. "Let's go to work."

The streets of Izmir were busy, but the view to the target's office from the roof was clear and direct. Tyrone peered through his nocs and found the top floor. "Seriously?" he asked.

"I know," Delaney said. "Doesn't look like much." The target was a fat middle-aged guy with greasy, stringy hair. He wore a dark suit and too much jewelry. He was talking to a younger guy, both of them gesticulating dramatically.

"Doesn't look like any arms dealer I've ever run across," Tyrone said.

Phillips dropped her nocs. "Let me explain something to you," she said. "Your mind is still on the battlefield. I get it, you're green again." He scowled at her, but she kept going. "This Wadjet thing is the next level. We're not going after ululating fanatics here. The bad guys we're chasing, they don't have horns or carry pitchforks."

"But that doesn't mean they're not bad guys," Delaney said. His hair was black, darker than their uniforms. He scratched it and went back to his nocs. "We chase the worst of the worst."

Tyrone paused. "But how can you be sure?" he asked.

Maxwell gave a quick look up, then went back to his binoculars. Phillips glowered at Tyrone. "When we get back," she said, "you need to have a talk with Brinkman."

They went back to watching. After a few moments, Maxwell moved closer to Tyrone. "Do you trust your doctor?" he asked, his voice low.

Tyrone dropped his nocs. "What?" he asked. "What are you talking about?"

Maxwell continued to watch. "Do you?"

Tyrone shook his head. "You guys are weird," he said.

"They're here," Jenkins said. Tyrone raised his nocs again. Two young women were being escorted into the office. T-shirts and blue jeans. The target rose and kissed them each on the cheek, then offered them cushioned chairs. "That's how we can be sure," Jenkins said. They gazed through their nocs, eyes locked on the target.

"Prostitution?" Tyrone asked, trying to hide his contempt. *Worst of the worst?*

"Trafficking," Delaney said. "Women from across eastern Europe."

"Where does he send them?" Tyrone asked.

"Where do you think?" Phillips said. "Places with bars on the windows. Guys who are too violent to get married for real. Brothels that confiscate their passports and make them work for decades to pay off the travel costs."

"Woah," Tyrone said. "That sucks." He watched the guy return to his desk and sit down. He pulled out a file from his desk and began sorting through papers.

"Yeah," Phillips said. "*That* is how we can be sure." She pulled the trigger and Tyrone froze as he watched the women run out of the room, screaming.

Tyrone stepped out of the elevator and down a long grey corridor of unmarked doors. Finally he reached Brinkman's reception area. Three guys sat in beige chairs, reading books while the secretary typed relentlessly into a computer. She looked up at him and gestured to a pair of huge thick doors.

Brinkman shook Tyrone's hand vigorously. "Welcome back," he said as he closed the doors. His DC office was three times the size of their operation in Tyrone's hometown. "Everything go okay in Izmir?"

"Yeah," Tyrone said, and waited. He glanced out the window at the midtown traffic. They were high up.

"Phillips said we should talk," he said, leaning forward and folding his hands. "First of all, I'm not mad. This is a different ball game."

"I'm fine," Tyrone said, his eyebrows tense.

Brinkman nodded and gave a slight smile. "I know," he said. "I wouldn't let you in if I thought there would be a problem." He paused. "But it's an adjustment. This isn't the usual routine."

Tyrone tilted his head. "Maybe not."

"And that's okay. It takes some getting used to."

Tyrone leaned in. "You know I trust you," he said.

"Of course," Brinkman said. "Like I trust my doctor." Tyrone raised an eyebrow and Brinkman smiled. "Do you know about my prostate cancer?"

Tyrone shook his head.

Brinkman waved a hand. "It's in remission," he said. "Don't worry, I'm fine. But I had to have docetaxel chemotherapy. Do you know anything about how that works?" Another head shake. "It disrupts the ability of cells to divide, which fights the spread of cancerous growths." He sighed. "It worked for me, but it was awful to go through. Vomiting, anemia, you feel weak all the time, your hair falls out. All that stuff."

"Sorry," Tyrone said.

Brinkman waved a hand. "Hey, whatever doesn't kill me, right?" Tyrone nodded. "Wadjet Squad is like that chemotherapy," Brinkman said. "It kinda sucks, having to trust someone who feeds that toxic crap into your arms. But if you don't, the cancer just grows and causes more suffering."

"Yeah," Tyrone said. "I got you."

Brinkman paused. "I hope so," he said. "Because some of these targets are going to look harmless." He waited. "But believe me, they are the cancer. And you're the chemotherapy. Do the work, avoid the strays, and then forget it." He pointed at Tyrone. "We're the good guys."

Phillips held up a photograph of a dumpy-looking white guy in his twenties. "Here he is," she said. "Get a good look."

Worst of the worst, Tyrone thought. He looked around at the rest of Wadjet Squad, huddled in the helicopter as they waited for the pilot. They were all dressed in civvies; this mission was low volume. "Who is he?" he asked.

"Brian Coleman," she said. "In three days he's planning to open fire on his college campus."

"Unless we stop him."

"That's right," she said. "We get a van in Denton, grab him on his way home from the bars, take him into the desert." She glanced around. "Any questions?"

Tyrone stared at the middle distance. Just one, but he wasn't going to ask. How do you find out about something like that? Why not let the cops deal with it? What if they got something wrong?

The pilot showed up. They took off and headed west.

Tyrone arrived at the *Parc de la Tête d'Or* before dawn. The nightmares were getting worse and he was lucky to get four hours of sleep a night. Still, the others were waiting for him on a bench near the lake. They were dressed down, covert weaponry beneath discreet uniforms.

He froze as he got close. "Where's Maxwell?" he asked.

Phillips looked up with an evil glare. "He's gone," she said. "Why do you care?"

Tyrone tilted his head. "I want to know who I'm working with," he said.

She raised a mocking eyebrow. "You know who you're working with," she said.

"Just four of us now?"

She stood up. "Five," she said with curt acid. "As always."

He glanced around. "So who's the fifth?"

"He'll be here in a minute." She sat down again.

Three minutes later Tyrone noticed a short guy walking toward them in their same uniform. He grinned and stood up.

"Ramirez!" he cried.

Ramirez grinned broadly, shook Tyrone's hand, and nodded to the others. "Phillips," he said. "Jenkins. Delaney." He had bulked up since Bali. He seemed calmer.

"How've you been?" Tyrone asked.

"Great," Ramirez said. "Let's get started."

They began surveillance on a bank executive. She was tall, with a deep love for grey business suits. For two days they followed her through tedious desk work and meetings about interest rates. They listened carefully for the name of her client with the chemical weapons, but the French was relentless and Tyrone was never really sure.

"There it is," Delaney said on the third morning.

"Are you sure?" Ramirez asked. "I didn't hear it."

"I did," Phillips said, standing up and pulling out the earbud. "Let's move."

Tyrone took a deep breath as he set the scope into position. Six hundred yards, light wind from the south. He glanced back at his new partner, a redhead named Hutchinson. If Phillips knew where Ramirez went, she wasn't talking.

"You really don't know?" Tyrone asked.

Hutchinson looked up from his nocs. "Know what?"

Tyrone sighed. "Why we're after this guy."

"I was hoping you knew."

Tyrone smiled. He tracked west and found Phillips and Delaney and Jenkins on the other cliff. Then he tracked back to the target. Middle-aged guy playing with his kids in the backyard of a house in the middle of a Montana cattle ranch.

"Maybe there's a weapons cache in the basement," Hutchinson said.

"Yeah," Tyrone said. "Maybe." *Worst of the worst*, he thought. *Chemotherapy*. He looked at Hutchinson again. "Do you trust your doctor?" he asked.

Hutchinson looked up, confused. "Huh?"

"Nothing. Never mind."

A burst of static came through the radio, followed by Phillips' voice. "Good a time as any," she said. "You want to do the honors?"

He looked at Hutchinson, who nodded hopefully. "Nah," he said. "I'm not feeling real confident today. You go ahead."

"If you insist," she said.

Two shots cracked the air and everything was silent again.

The streets of Choloma were crowded and noisy and hot. Tyrone wiped at his forehead as he pulled out the chair and sat down across from Ramirez.

Ramirez smiled. "The fact that I saw you coming means you're not here to take me out," he said. "I hope."

Tyrone shook his head. "No," he said. "Nothing like that. How you doing?"

Ramirez looked around and took a sip of his lime soda. "You know how I'm doing," he said. "Four hours of sleep a night if I'm lucky."

Tyrone nodded. "Nightmares?"

Ramirez sighed. "All the time. You?"

Tyrone nodded again and glanced at the street. "Why Honduras?"

Ramirez smiled. "My family's from here, man. My cousin lives over there." He pointed to the north.

Tyrone leaned onto the table. "What was it?" he asked. "How is this any different from before?"

He paused, the bottle at his lips. "What, are you joking?" Tyrone shook his head. "Oh, you're joking." Ramirez drank. "How is it different?" He set the bottle down. "Man, how do you think they find these people? Who are we dealing with?" Tyrone stared into the middle distance. "Brinkman? You trust that guy?" Tyrone didn't answer. "He gave you the speech about cancer too, right? 'Do you trust your doctor?' That whole thing?"

"And?"

He spread his hands. "So who decides these guys are the worst of the worst? And how?"

"C'mon," Tyrone said, unsure of his words. "They get intel—"

"You know what I heard?" Ramirez leaned in close. "I heard there's some weird goddamned ritual they do where they drink snake's blood." His eyes were wide. "I mean, yeah, they get intel on terrorists and arms dealers. But come on — Brian Coleman? How do you predict a shooting spree on a college campus?" Tyrone shrugged. "And if you got something, why not go to the cops? What the hell does Kr have to do with it?"

Tyrone sat back and watched the traffic. Horns blew in the smoggy air.

"I'm telling you," Ramirez said. "They're trying to play God."

Tyrone watched the traffic.

"That stuff don't turn out good," Ramirez said, sitting back. "I'm done."

Tyrone sighed. "Yeah," he said. "I think I am too."

Hutchinson checked his M4 and glanced at Phillips. "Where's the fifth?" he asked. Even the helicopter pilot was geared up and ready to go. "He's late. I like to know who I'm working with."

"I'm not late," Brinkman said, hopping into the chopper. "You're just early."

"You're coming with us?" Hutchinson asked.

Brinkman smiled. "This mission is special," he said, strapping in. "I don't want to miss the fun."

"Where are we going?" Hutchinson asked as the pilot started the engine.

"Honduras," Brinkman shouted. "We've got a couple of intel liabilities to take care of."

Lost Track

for Chinny and Stu

To entire sincerity there belongs ceaselessness.

Confucius

My hands sank into something plastic and squishy. I made a grotesque face as I felt my fingers move around the thick nasty whatever it was. I imagined a diaper filled with diarrhea, or a grocery bag full of raccoon intestines. I wished I wasn't wearing my favorite green hoodie.

"Eww!" I said, then immediately closed my mouth and fought back some heaving from my stomach. The stench of trash and vomit and garbage and filth and putrescence was everywhere. I could feel it seeping into my sneakers, winding through my hair, billowing into my hoodie.

Serena was face-down in the muck to my right. A swarm of flies droned around each of us, darting about as we sifted through the city's trash. Mounds of garbage surrounded us on every side. She spit again, a disgusting line of brown slobber flying from her lips.

"Are you chewing again?"

She shrugged. "Just a little. It's keeping me focused." Another spit, in my direction.

"Gross!" I said. "Aim that crap somewhere else." I pulled a blue gym bag out of the slime and unzipped it, then recoiled from the gruesome new stench of death and old meat. I tried again to hold back the puke, but my stomach was gripping my whole throat and pushing its way into my mouth. I turned to the side and watched breakfast spew across a black garbage bag. I groaned and wiped at my face with my arm.

It's funny what good music will do to you.

When they had first started dating, Serena's boyfriend Chad made a mix disc for her, filled with stuff she liked and stuff he hoped she'd like. Some of it was way off-base, but one of the tracks was just glorious. We listened to it over and over and over. Five times a day for weeks. The beat was electric, both literally and figuratively. An AK-47 with sick grooving keys all around it and this pitchshifted vocal that fit perfectly. The kind of thing you have to turn the volume up on, then just keep turning it up, because it's never loud enough. Like the first time I heard "Hive" from Rogue Element. Only better.

Problem was, we never bothered to learn what the song was called, or who made it. We looked on the silly little CD cover he'd made, but it had some long, complicated title that we would never remember. Normally I would immediately hunt down more info on the band, so I could find more of their stuff. But at the time I was worried with "Chad's Track" (as we called it) that their other songs wouldn't be as good, so we just let it be what it was. And now, here we were.

After the breakup Serena began chewing tobacco. It was really weird for her, totally out of character. She was a chocoholic with a passion for sugary kids' cereals. She said something once about how he made fun of her for never doing anything dangerous, so I guessed the chewing was a weird act of defiance or something. People do weird things when love breaks apart.

She also threw out a lot of his stuff. Burned some of it. Gave some of it back. And then we realized that the CD had been in one of those piles. She was pretty sure it was the one we'd thrown out. So here we were, plowing through acres of dog feces and rancid leftovers, praying that the next pile would bring us back to that heavenly beat.

"I'm starting to wonder if this is really worth it," Serena said, letting fly another globby brown stream. She gestured toward me. "You're puking, I'm getting sick, and I'm hungry as all hell."

"Twenty more minutes," I said. "Then we'll call it a day." I turned around and dipped back into a mound of garbage. Suddenly I noticed an old pizza box from Doughey's and gave a little shriek.

"What?" Serena asked, whirling to see me hop over to it. I waved the box in the air and she joined me. We were the only people we knew who ordered from Doughey's. Their pizza sucked, but it was cheap. Sure enough, the box heralded a bag of our own trash. I ripped open the black plastic and flung aside old electric bills and banana peels. Finally, at the bottom, I hit paydirt. I pulled a short stack of case-less discs out of the muck and held them aloft. I let the first two fall back into the garbage, and grinned like an idiot as I finally set eyes on Chad's Mix.

We raced back to the car. "It was track four," I said, fumbling with my keys as Serena wiped the disc on her sleeve.

"No way," she said. "It was six." We sank into the seats and I ejected Daft Punk from the CD player. Serena gave me a hesitant look. "You think it might screw up your stereo?" she asked.

"I don't care," I said, pushing her hand and forcing the disc inside. "It'll be worth it." For several tense seconds, we watched the display blink "reading" at us. Then it kept blinking. "Uh oh," I said. Not a good sign. More blinking. "Dammit!" I said, banging the steering wheel. The display switched to "error" and ejected the disc.

Serena slumped back in her seat. "The stereo is sticking its tongue out at us," she said.

The door of the dryer opened with a clank and I pulled my head back, recoiling from the fumes. I clenched my teeth violently and half-grunted, half-screamed a very bad word. I sank to my knees, the rough stone basement floor digging in through the denim.

Serena looked over from the tiny little desk where she was drawing a comic strip. "No good?" she asked.

I batted the dryer door weakly. It swung toward the latch, but remained open. "This sucks," I replied. "Now they smell like garbage, butt, filth, *and* fabric softener." Even worse, the CD had refused to cooperate with any of the players we'd tried: her portable, my computer, the GameBox 420. Serena read somewhere that baking a CD in the oven might help, so she tried that. All we got was a nasty new smell in the oven.

She approached, and put up a hand when she came into stink range. "Oh, yegods," she said. "Same crap, but now it's covered with bleach and perfume."

I sighed. "And don't just make it worse by covering it up with some Right Guard," I sang. She'd never been a De La fan, but the reference made me smile anyway. But I was still pissed. "That's my favorite hoodie in there," I said, and looked up at her. "Any luck with the boots?"

"Nope," she said. She'd been spraying them with harsh cleansers and hot water every day for a week. "I don't think we've got many options left."

"This sucks," I said again. She walked back to her tiny desk and spat into an old coffee can. "Guh!" I cried. "That is too gross for words," I put a hand to my stomach. "Like I wasn't sick to my guts already." I sighed. "You have got to give that up."

She shrugged. "When the time is right," she said. "Meantime, what are we going to do with this stuff?" She gestured to the dryer, the stench wafting out of the crack in the door. My gaze wandered around the basement, my nose still clenched in a disgusted wrinkle.

"We've gotta do something," I said. "The dryer is already coated in that stink." Another sigh. "That was my favorite hoodie," I said again. I could see the sleeve through the crack in the door. "We've been through so much together." I was only sort of joking.

Serena nodded absently. "We gotta just throw it all away," she said. "Never look back." Then she froze. "No, wait." She bolted upstairs and came back a minute later with a paper grocery sack. She held her breath and shoved the nasty garbage clothes into the bag.

"Actual unretouched photo of sack," I said.

She stopped rolling the top shut and gave me a look. "What the fudge is that?"

I waved a hand and smiled. "Inside joke."

She tilted her head down at me. "I've told you before — inside jokes are pointless unless you're telling them to someone who *knows what you're talking about!*" She gave the bag a shake and said "Come on," then started up the stairs. I followed along. Up in the kitchen she opened the oven, grabbed Chad's mix disc, and dropped it into the bag.

Outside, she picked up her boots — dripping with cleanser and water — and jammed them into the bag. She motioned for me to open the trunk of my car and dumped the bulging mass inside. "Come on," she said again, climbing into the passenger seat.

I got in and started it up. "Where to?" She directed me to the gas station two streets way, then went inside. She returned two minutes later with a shiny red plastic gas container. She pulled a nozzle out from the pump and filled the container with gas, then banged on the trunk. I opened it up and she put the gas inside, then returned to the passenger seat.

"You remember that warehouse I dragged you to last year?" she asked. "Where Chad and I used to go for those weird picnics?"

"Yeah."

"Take me there." She rolled down the window and spat into the parking lot as I pulled away.

The warehouse was huge. Possibly an old factory or assembly line. An ancient husk of postindustrial decay, it must have been 80 years old. Brown paint peeling under layers of rusting rust. Gaping holes where windows had been smashed away decades ago. A cavernous floor, with big swinging doors that no longer cared about keeping anything out or in. Clumps of heavy metal barrels sat in one corner, with a weird orange ooze pooled on the ground among them. Dirt and grime lay upon the floor like a sickly carpet.

I kicked a tin can, hard. It clattered a few feet and lay dead again, less than a third of the way across the floor. "You came here for *picnics*?" I asked.

Serena nodded. "Yeah, Chad said he liked the feel of this place." She walked slowly toward the opposite wall, clutching the grocery sack in one hand, gas can in the other. "Something about how it was so big and powerful, but so empty."

I nodded. "That's deep, man."

"Yeah, well." She spat, the splattery gob of brown sauce blending perfectly into the disgusting floor. "He was a deep guy."

I saw some tiny rodent bones up against a wall, partially covered by a small chips bag with an old design on it. "Eww!" I said. "Freakin' rat bones."

Serena jogged over to where I was grimacing at the remains. "Woah," she said, and spat carefully, to avoid disturbing the gravesite. "I remember that old logo for Salt Doodles." We gazed for a few seconds at the bizarre combination of snacks and rats.

"Can you imagine?" I said eventually. "You die, your body rots, you get eaten by maggots and whatever. And then someone comes and eats some potato chips and tosses the bag on top of your final resting place, and it just stays there."

Serena nodded. "Yeah, and then your bones *and* the Doodles bag become part of some sad hollow ghost building."

"Yeah," I said. "Your bones are buried by the bag, but both you and the bag are buried by time."

"It's like we came from one garbage dump to another."

I shook my head. "No way, man. Garbage dumps are nasty, but they're *alive*. Just because you throw it away doesn't mean it's dead."

Serena nodded. "Yeah, you're right." She took a deep breath and spat, then gave the grocery sack a shake. "Speaking of which." She flung the sack in front of us. The boots tried to push out through the rolled-up top, but gave up and lay still. Serena flipped the cap off the gas can and the popping noise bounced off the walls. She jiggled the gasoline over the bag, splashing oily liquid everywhere. It sank into the brown paper, coursing over the boulder-shaped package. Rivulets of gasoline ran over the edges and drifted toward the doors, trying to escape the impending blaze. The last few drops dripped around, and she chucked the can behind us.

She spat on the bag. "You suck, Chad," she said. "The only good thing you ever gave me was that song."

I nodded. "And we can't even listen to it." I hocked phlegm from the back of my throat and spat on the bag, too. I wanted it to have some sort of meaning, but I was really just clearing my throat. Chad had never done me wrong, but I was angry for how he treated Serena.

She took a lighter out of her pocket, a miniature plastic piece of junk she'd probably bought at the gas station. She knelt down to one of the gasoline tendrils drifting away from the bag, flicked the lighter, and set the flame into the puddle. I expected it to meander toward the sack like that scene in *The Usual Suspects*, but instead it all seemed to flare up at once.

I stepped back as a nasty cloud of garbage-smelling black smoke puffed up and blew toward us. The fire was also creeping, as gasoline continued to spread away, so I took another step back and expected Serena to do the same. But instead she just stood there, watching the fire consume her boots and our clothing. The puddle of gas crawled up to her shoes, but turned away when it got there.

The stench got really nasty, like the flame was unleashing some primordial evil that had seeped into our clothes. *Why didn't my green hoodie smell nice as it passed into the next world?* I wondered. We had had some fantastic times, experiences that surely infused it with warm memories of happiness and sunshine. I put my right arm over my face and tried not to breathe. But Serena just stood there, as though her olfactories had gone dead. "Dude," I said finally. "Back up. Your clothes are going to smell like that nasty garbage again." But she didn't move.

Instead, she pulled the can of chewing tobacco from her back pocket and gazed at it. The light of the flames danced on it. "This is still the first can," she said. "I bought it the day he took off." She took the lid off and shook a few loose pieces toward the fire. "Now it's all gone."

I nodded and rolled my eyes a little. How clichéd. "I guess this is the right time, huh?"

She put a finger in her mouth and pulled the wad of sloppy brown-black goop out, and flung it into the fire. Then she dropped the can on top. It clattered over the smoldering ashes and fell onto the floor, undamaged. She kicked the can back into the ashes and moved the pile of crap around. The last licks of flame were dying out, and she spat one last time onto the mess.

Then she pulled a new can of tobacco out of her front pocket and undid the plastic tape. She took the lid off and drew out a pinch, then pushed it into her lip. "I guess not," she said, and began walking toward the car.

Monday, 7:37 AM. Slouched in barely-padded mismatched chairs at RealWork Incorporated. Smell of oily coffee waving through the air, surrounded by people just like us. Waiting. Wasting our time.

The front desk looked like a fast-food counter. It probably was, once upon a time. I can totally see booths lining the walls and windows where the brick is now. We might as well be using trays. Here you are today. Throw the assignment away when you're done. Come back tomorrow, get something new that's totally the same.

In a way, temping ought to be fun. The first day of work is always fun — you get to meet new people, be in a new environment, adjust to a new schedule. But after about three weeks, I realized that the minute differences from place to place meant nothing. The crushing similitude deflated me. Perky receptionist, meaningless filing, inane rules that I wouldn't be around long enough to get punished for disobeying. Overqualified for the heavy lifting that paid better, underqualified for the positions that might become full-time.

I was flipping through the latest copy of *Newsweek*. News for rich people. Wall street. Washington. Business deals. Trade agreements. Environmental innovations. Eventually I started ignoring the articles and went back to page one, to examine the ads. Skinny happy people and shiny new stuff. It was all fake, of course, but it was also all transient. It came, and then it went. This lady in the toothpaste ad — where was she now? Not being the poster child for toothpaste, surely. Was she posing for some clothing catalogue? Or had she moved on to real acting?

The bark of the secretary snapped me out of it. "Vizcaino," she called, not looking up from her clipboard. God, how I hated that stupid clipboard. Like it was attached to her hand or something. Serena gave me a look and traipsed up to the counter. I heard something about an office on the north side. She came back toward me clutching a job slip.

"It's on Sherman," she said languidly, pinching some chew into her lip. "I can take the bus."

"Nah, it's okay," I said, grabbing my jacket from the chair beside me. "I need to get outta here." We went outside and got in the car and took off.

She rolled the window down and spat. "I can't keep doing this," she said. "I need something stable."

I nodded and fiddled with my music player, swapping my attention between it and the road. "Yeah," I said. "I know what you mean. I think I'm gonna go back to Hauger's."

She was slouched in the seat, a hand to her eyes. "That crazy guy still the manager?"

"I dunno," I said. "I heard he's gotten better." I finally got sick of looking and just hit shuffle. TMBG came on, and we both made the whip-cracking motion. "But I don't even care. He's not as bad as this constant back and forth."

We waited for the light to change. "It's one thing to hate the place you work," she said. "But how weird is it to hate a place where we don't even work?"

"We hate the place where we wait to work."

She gave a weak little not-laugh, hollow with desperation. "Yeah." She watched the world go by for a minute. "Nothing stays."

She was quoting Cyberaktif, 1990. Where was I? I didn't hear it when it first came out. I sang a line from the chorus. "A message .. to you, how I feel .." I paused. "Do you think they meant that to be comforting?" I asked. So long ago.

She stared out the window, then stared some more. "Does it matter?" she said finally.

There's a point where the bass drum moves beyond thump into pound. It's to do with the size and construction of the speaker, it's to do with the architecture of the track. And it's to do with where you play it.

We were in the perfect place for pounding bass, but the guy running the system knew enough to keep from overdoing it. The big open space let the bass pound, without drowning in its own distortion. I was sweating too much, moving too much, but I couldn't help it. It was Crystal Method doing Daft Punk from *Tron Legacy*. Serena gave me a look and gestured to my sweaty armpits. I knew she couldn't hear me, but maybe she could read my lips. "It's the music," I said, the evangelical via Meat Beat Manifesto. "It's the music." I think she recognized it, or maybe she just smiled because I was being silly. Then she looked back at the DJ.

There wasn't much to see — just a guy in a baseball cap — but she'd been looking at him all night. I got close enough for her to hear. "Go talk to him!" I yelled.

She looked back again at the clutch of ladies around him. "Tell me you don't see those Snookis all over him," she yelled.

"But they're *Snookis*," I yelled. More pounding bass. "And he doesn't seem interested." He was frowning at the decks. *Besides*, I thought, *Snooki wouldn't know Crystal Method from crystal meth*.

But she shook her head again and made a drinking hand gesture and went toward the beverage tables. Then I heard the opening line "rock the house in" of the Crystal Method on Prodigy's "Voodoo People" and I nearly pissed myself. I looked toward the DJ because he'd just jumped two notches on the cool meter, but then I realized he was teasing me. It was just the first sound bit. No one else probably even realized what they'd heard, he'd mixed it in so well. He put it in again, as some other beat fell on top, and faded it out with the *Tron*. But he was going to bring it back, I knew it.

I wandered toward the beverage tables and saw Serena at the door, gazing into the night. I watched her for a second, then gagged as she spat onto the concrete. I turned away and got some water and walked over to her. "What up?" she said, not looking at me. "You thought this was Voodoo People."

"I totally did," I said. "He'll play it next, watch."

"Probably."

"Serena, I'm serious. Give me a reason why you won't talk to him."

She gave that desperate weak not-laugh again. "I don't have anything to say to him."

I sighed. "You're my friend so I don't mind telling you this," I said. "But I'm getting sick of listening to you." I drank. "And that means that you're probably sick of listening to yourself."

"I try not to listen to myself these days," she said.

I drank again. The water was cold. I spilled a little in my hand and rubbed it on my forehead. "Hey," I said, looking around. "This isn't the place where we .." I made a little burning motion.

"No," she said, and spat, then gestured with her drink. "I think it's over there." She began walking. "Let's see what survived."

We peered into two different warehouses before we found the one with our charred sack remains. The streetlight barely lit the area around it. I sighed as I realized I was looking at the singed sleeve of my favorite hoodie. We stood for a second in silence. Suddenly Serena nudged me and gestured silently into the darkness. I made out someone crumpled up in the corner, then realized it was two people.

"Oh gross," I whispered. "Are they..?"

"Yeah, they're totally making out. Let's go."

We made it back to the party and felt the music wrap itself back around us. "He's gonna play it soon," I said, and kicked a cup. "We need to figure out what you're gonna say to your DJ crush." She stopped walking and gave me a look. "Oh come on," I said. "That was pretty good." She reached into her mouth and pulled out the slimy glob of tobacco and flung it toward me. I stepped out of the way just as "Voodoo People" came on for real. I dropped my cup and water spilled everywhere and I jogged to the floor in between the stupid people who didn't realize what they were hearing and then there was nothing but me and the tinny beat and the whirling synths and that bassline swarmed in and then the drums started pounding and it was everything and I was lost in the oblivion of the beat and I kept moving and feeling it and it was awesome and three minutes later I looked up and there was Serena, just as lost as me and I almost cried because it was such a perfect moment and we kept dancing and smiling and then something else came into the song that I didn't recognize and I stopped moving because I realized that I *did* recognize it and then I actually did start crying a little bit because Serena stopped and she looked at me too and her eyes widened and I knew that she knew and then she turned and walked straight for the DJ and I followed her.

She didn't exactly elbow a Snooki out of the way, but the girl gave her a look like she had. Serena saw a notepad where the DJ had scrawled a bunch of track names and times. She moved toward it and he yelled "Hey!" and she made a writing motion and he shrugged a little and nodded toward it. She turned a page and took his pen and wrote: "Please give me the name of this song." Then she showed it to him. He put the headphones into his shoulder and took the pen and wrote: "It's got a crazy long title." She took the pad back and wrote: "I know. This is really important. Can I wait and see the record?" He smiled when she showed him, and then he wrote: "Yeah. Or give me your email and I'll send it to you." *I won't laugh I won't laugh I won't laugh*. She smiled and tried to ignore me and said "yeah" but he didn't hear her, but I did. She wrote her email address down and then tore it off and handed it to him. He nodded with a little smile of his own and took out his wallet and put her address in it.

She turned and pulled the can of chew out of her pocket and handed it to me. I raised an eyebrow and she nodded. *Finally*. We waited until the song ended, and she turned to a new page on the pad and he pulled the disc off the turntable and showed the label to her. She scribbled furiously and smiled at him. "Thanks!" she yelled as the new song came to life.

"You don't trust me?" he yelled.

She shrugged. "Stuff happens," she yelled. "I can't take any more chances with this track." She hesitated and folded the paper and handed it to me. "How about this," she yelled to him as I put it in my pocket. "If I don't hear from you, I can get it from her."

He nodded and we turned to go. Then I stopped and stepped to him. "Thanks for the Crystal Method," I yelled. He smiled and nodded, then turned back to the music.

When we were in the parking lot, I threw her the keys. "You drive," I said. "I'm worn out." We climbed in and she started up the car. I reached over and fiddled with the music player. I found the Cs and Cyberaktif came on.

We listened for a minute. Then she said: "I guess it's comforting."

Imposition

for Christie and Garrett

```
                          •   •
                          3.  4.

                          •   •
                          11. 12.

                          •   •
                          19. 20.

                          •   •
                          27. 28.

 •    •    •    •    •   •    •    •    •    •
 2.   10.  18.  26.  33. 34.  29.  21.  13.  5.
 •    •    •    •    •   •    •    •    •    •
 1.   9.   17.  25.  36. 35.  30.  22.  14.  6.

                          •   •
                          32. 31.


                          •   •
                          24. 23.


                          •   •
                          16. 15.


                          •   •
                          8.  7.
```

Scientists often object to the concept of God on the grounds that it explains the universe too easily: You can't see how it "works." God is a contextual Theory of Everything. But a reductionist Theory of Everything suffers from the same problem. The physicist's belief that the mathematical laws of a Theory of Everything really do govern every aspect of the universe is very like a priest's belief that God's laws do. The main difference is that the priest is looking outward while the physicist looks inward. Both are offering an interpretation of nature; neither can tell you how it works.

Jack Cohen and Ian Stewart
The Collapse of Chaos: Discovering Simplicity in a Complex World

"My god," I said, staring at the headline. "Kim, listen to this."

It was Monday evening, around dusk. That time of day when afternoon blends like cream into nightfall's coffee; when the pressures of the day gently subside, slowly replaced by the pressures of the night.

I had nothing to do on Tuesday. I decided to take the night off. There's an intoxicating sense of freedom that comes on the evening before a day away from responsibilities. When all is said and done, the night before is the real time off. Sundays are only sort of free; you have to go to bed early, maybe do homework. If you're one of *those* people, you have to go to church. And besides, weekends are usually housework days. Cleaning, laundry, repair, lawn, grocery shopping. Some day off.

But today was a real day off. There was nothing I had to worry about. The work I'd done that day just lifted away as I sat there in the living room with Kim, reading the newspaper. I was in the recliner, my blue journal and a pen asleep on the small table in front of me. I'd done some writing earlier, but after several awkward starts I threw in the towel.

Now I wanted to let my mind be empty, to enjoy the sense of nullity that could come with a day of vacation. Kim was headed in the same direction, I knew, but even more so — she had Tuesdays *and* Wednesdays off. She was stretched out on the sofa, reading a book.

She looked over at me. "What?"

"Two kids were shot to death in Littleton, Colorado," I said. "In a Subway."

"Littleton has a subway system?"

"No, the restaurant."

"Oh."

"Check this out." I read from the news report. "'I hope it was just a robbery,' said one of Kunselman's co-workers.. 'I've had more than enough of this. This stuff needs to stop.' How bizarre is that? To be hoping that a friend of yours was killed because of a robbery."

"If it's better than the alternative.."

"That's so horrible," I said, and read some more. "Hmm. They listed all these things that have happened since the Columbine shootings, and then this guy who went to the scene of the killing to bring flowers said: 'Every week, there's something that happens here.. This is supposed to be a normal community.'"

"Phh," Kim said. "There's no such thing."

"What do you mean?"

"What *is* a 'normal community?' Is it a perfect little suburb where soccer moms take their kids around in minivans and cheerful dads come home after a long day at the office and play with their children and everyone grows up happy, respecting each other and loving everything? Please. That doesn't exist. It's a fairy tale.

"When the massacre first happened," she went on, "what was the first thing out of the mouths of everyone there?" She looked up at me.

I blinked. "What?"

"'How could this have happened here?'" she said, with mock hysteria. "'This is such a nice community. What went wrong? Littleton is normal. This is a normal school. This isn't supposed to happen here.' Which means, of course, that it's supposed to happen somewhere. The kids and parents are used to hearing about this sort of thing. But not where *they* live. Black and Latino kids have gang fights; we're used to hearing about that. But rich white kids aren't supposed to shoot each other. That's an abnormality. More fairy tales. It's as if we're saying that the rationale and mindset behind the use of violence reaches some of our kids, but not others.

"Well, which is worse? To believe that this is intentional, or not? Which is more horrifying? To say that we teach all kids that violence is okay, and some kids understand that we don't really mean it, and some don't? Or to say that our society purposely teaches some kids that violence is okay, so that they take each other out, and shows other kids — the kids in the 'normal' communities — that violence is not acceptable? Frankly, I don't know which scenario is more frightening."

"Which do you think it is?" I asked.

"I don't think it's either of them," she said. "It's not about normal or not normal communities; like I said, there's no such thing. Normal is about standards, typical states. Normal means what's usual. Well, in our world, violence is usual. It's very usual. More than that, even. It's the trump card. It's how things get done. It's like Mao said: 'Power grows from the barrel of a gun.'"

"But there are other kinds of power."

"Sure there are. But none are more efficient, more final, more certain than violence. And more to the point, none have been used as much through history as violence."

I had closed the paper. "So are you saying there's an inherent tendency in humans toward violence?"

She smiled and shook her head. "Not at all. But we're very quick to use it, and it's what most people see in the world. It's the way decisions are made. If two countries have a dispute, they go to war. If two men in a bar disagree, chances are they'll fight about it."

"Yeah, but a lot of people go to court instead, or settle the problem peacefully."

"True. But that's a very recent development. And besides, it's often seen as a coward's solution. Can't stand up for yourself? Go run to the cops. That's the main idea of our modern era — standing up for oneself, being self-reliant, defending one's home and family. Or in some cases, one's gang, or street or what have you. Someone who can do those things — and it requires violence — is considered a 'real' man. It's usually about manhood, but plenty of women think that way, too. You have to be able

161

to stand up for yourself, or you're spineless, you're weak. This usually takes the form of bloodless power plays, but behind it rests the lever of violence."

"How do you mean?"

"Let's take the boss and the worker. If you're a worker, and you constantly let the boss dump on you, you'll start to feel bad about yourself. It doesn't help, of course, that your co-workers are probably also giving you shit about not standing up for yourself. So you can have a power struggle with your boss, where you make him look stupid every now and then, or make jokes about his wife, or whatever. But the boss can respond by cutting your hours, or lowering your wage. After all, the boss is the one in charge. If things really come to a head, you can get fired. And there's nothing you can do about that. Because if you refuse to leave, the boss can have the police come and escort you out. After all, it's their property.

"Which brings us to the key point about the use of violence: It's usually used by the wealthy to keep the folks below quiet. The police, for all their good work in building community and keeping the streets safe, are mainly there to protect the property of the people who own the country. If you don't own anything, the police aren't likely to be on your side."

"But they just enforce the laws," I said.

"Right. And who wrote the laws? Look, don't get me wrong. There are a lot of laws that have been established to protect the rights of poor people. But that came from long and — ironically enough — violent struggle. What you end up with is a system that provides recourse for people who don't own a lot, but is still based on the idea that those who own the place make the rules. And how come they own the place?"

"Well, they say property is theft."

"Right, exactly. Someone had to say, once upon a time, 'This is mine.' They were probably talking about land. Land, incidentally, that had the best resources: food, metal, whatever. Well, enforcing that requires the use of violence. Because someone's going to try to challenge you on it. They'll say, 'No, it isn't. It's mine.'"

"Maybe they'll say 'This land belongs to all of us, you can't claim it.'"

She nodded. "Maybe. But not too many people are willing to die for that. Especially if there's another plot of land nearby that will work as well for such a purpose. Either way, you eventually get a bunch of people who all claim to own parts of the land. And some parts are more bountiful than others. And some parts have better shelter. And maybe one part of the land is considered 'holy.' So *everyone* claims to own that part. But when all is said and done, it's all just made up."

"It's totally arbitrary."

"Yeah. Whoever has the biggest stick wins. Might makes right. *That's* what kids learn. That's what we teach ourselves to believe. And just as important, we teach ourselves that there's no other way things could possibly be. We learn that the way things are is the way things must be. And as a boon to the system, we learn that the current structure works so well that any different path would be a disaster. We have to keep going the way we're going, or the world will come to an end."

I gestured to the article. "Sometimes it seems like the world *is* coming to an end."

She smiled. "Exactly."

"Is it?" The paper was closed now. We moved around as we talked.

"I don't know," she said. "I don't think I have access to enough evidence — I don't think anyone does — to say. There's probably as much evidence for as there is against. In either case, that's really just a figure of speech. 'The world's coming to an end.' We don't really mean that a careful assessment of the available factors suggests a trend in that direction."

"Some people do."

"Yeah, okay. They do. But they're just imposing their vision of the world on what's around them. A vision, by the way, that suits their political or religious or social agenda. Besides, what does it mean for the world to come to an end? Do you mean the planet Earth will cease to exist? Or that humankind will be eliminated? Or just that our institutions will crumble and dissolve? The questions you ask make a big difference in the answers you get."

"Sure they do. But we all do that, don't we? We're all just looking for the truth that underlies it all. To see the objective reality that's behind the processes around us."

She shook her head vigorously. "No," she said. "There's no such thing. If that's what you're shooting for, you're wasting your time."

"You don't think there's such a thing as truth?" I asked.

"Look," she said. "The only order that exists in the universe is the one we dream up for it. It's all just an imposed order. That's all religion is. Same with the grand unification theory. And all this stuff we've got nowadays about angels. Things happen for reasons, but the reasons don't make sense in any ultimate framework. If it seems like they do, that's just because the reasons in question are convenient for that framework. If you do something wrong, and then something bad happens to you, that's not God's hand or karma — it's a coincidence! Period. Did you ever read Philip K. Dick's book *VALIS*?"

I nodded. "Yeah."

"Do you remember that part about the cat? Why did it get killed? Because it got hit by a car. Why did it get hit by a car? Because it was in the street at the same time as a car. Why? Only the cat knows. Maybe it was chasing a bird. Maybe it was running windsprints. We can dream up a beautiful and plausible design for how the universe operates, but when it comes right down to it, it just does. It does what it does, without regard to morality or justice or even life itself. To hell with life. Life doesn't mean a thing to this universe. It doesn't care if we live or die."

"So then why shouldn't I kill you right now?"

She raised a finger. "Ah. Why, indeed?"

"Well?" I asked.

"Because being dead not only cuts me off from any future actions I may have wanted to take, but it causes untold misery and suffering among my friends and family."

"And the action may come back to haunt me. Or your friends and family might seek revenge."

"Let's say it doesn't, and they don't. So what? Is the prevention of misery not worthwhile in itself?"

"Of what intrinsic value is the prevention of misery?" I asked. "Especially if it means discomfort — or misery — for me?"

"There's nothing intrinsically valuable about it," she said. "Not for you. But that value's relative. You always have to put yourself in the other person's shoes. Into other people's."

"But why? What good will it do me? If my success is based on doing whatever I need to do, then putting myself in their shoes will only set me back."

"Well, that all depends on what you mean by success."

"Reaching my goals."

"Which are?"

"The main one is: Be happy. Content — not just mindlessly joyous. At peace."

"Those are all very different things. But then the question is: What do those things require?"

"Sometimes they require my *not* thinking of others."

"Why?"

"Because resources are scarce. Someone wants to take my land. Like you said."

She waved a hand. "Nonsense. There are enough resources for everyone. It may require us to cut down on the number of SUVs and diamond rings in the world, but it is possible for humans to reach a sustainable balance with the planet."

"How about with each other?"

She nodded. "That's a little trickier, but it's possible."

"Fine then. Let's approach it from another direction. How can I feel at peace when I have so much and others have so little? How can I sleep at night if I'm thinking of starving kids?"

"What should you be doing besides sleeping?"

"Working to get food to them."

"But it'll never be enough."

"You just said—"

"No, I mean that you'll be up against tremendously powerful institutions that are designed to keep the kids hungry. You're one person. You can spend your nights without sleep, trying to get food to starving kids. But you're swimming upstream."

"Well, that all depends on how much food I can get. Besides, I'll know I did what I could."

"But maybe you could do more the next day if you were well-rested."

"That's a rationalization."

"No, it's the big picture."

"Does the little picture count at all?"

"Of course it does — that's all we have in the present tense. But it's not all there is. And we have the ability to pause and look at the big picture."

I nodded. "Yeah, but we also have the ability to abuse the big picture."

"Of course we do. But that doesn't mean we shouldn't see it. The possibility of arson shouldn't eliminate campfires."

I paused. "But isn't the big picture just another kind of imposed order? How much proof is there that your big picture is correct, and the New Testament is wrong?"

"Because," she said. "It's cause and effect, with statistics and reality. It's a science."

"But Christians claim the same things about the Bible. Try to convince Billy Graham that God's not real. His God."

"Sure he's real. To Billy Graham. Again, it's relative." She scratched her nose. "It's also a delusion."

"Well, maybe this big picture of yours is a delusion too."

"Yeah, maybe it is."

I nodded and smirked.

"But if you can prove that it is," she said, "I'm willing to admit it."

"Billy Graham would say the same thing."

"Yeah, but how do you prove that God isn't real? You can't prove to me that the tooth fairy doesn't exist. Besides, if my big picture is a delusion, then that means that those starving kids are a delusion, too."

"Not necessarily. Because there are starving kids in the New Testament. The question is, what's behind them? Why are they there?"

"And what does the New Testament say about that? It says: 'Render unto Caesar what is Caesar's.' There will always be poor people. Are you kidding me?"

"Well, there are all kinds of big pictures. And who's to say that one is more valid than another?"

"Because one says that horrible suffering is okay — notice it's not usually preached by those who are doing the suffering, but that's another story — and one says it's not only unacceptable, but completely unnecessary."

"That's a value judgment."

"Sure it is. And I'm making it. But it's a judgment based on human lives, and pain, and justice. Not on some arbitrary system of morality that comes from a really old book."

"The more you talk about this big picture, the more it sounds like a religion."

"It's not—"

"Okay, okay. It sounds like an imposed system of order."

"It's not. It's an image, an idea. That's all. It doesn't go off and explain all sorts of things, and it certainly doesn't speculate as to why things are the way they are."

"But we can make some educated guesses in that direction, can't we? I mean, kids are starving because they don't have access to food. Right?"

She nodded. "And why don't they have access to food?"

"Because wealthy people don't want to give up their opulent lifestyles."

"They're greedy."

"That's one way of putting it."

"Fine. And why are they greedy?"

"Because. . . ." I hesitated.

She nodded. "See, that's where we hit the snag. There are all kinds of reasons why people are the way they are. And it makes some sense to try to figure out what those reasons are. But there's no one answer to it all."

"Look," I said. "Our actions have consequences. Even far-reaching consequences. So far that we can't really predict them. But as far as we can, we need to be aware of them."

"Fine. No one's arguing that."

"And for those we can't see, we have to make an educated guess."

"Why?"

Imposition

"Because—"

"Look," she said. "Don't we have our hands full already, looking at what we *can* see? Why do we have to go around worrying about things we can't see? You get preachers more worried about the eternal soul of the homeless guy than the fact that the guy's starving to death."

"Okay, but it sounds like you're trying to say that we can't see some things. What about analyzing systems and institutions?"

"What about it?"

"Is it worthless?"

"Who said it was?"

"Order is meaningless, you said. It doesn't exist."

"In the universe, I said. Big, grandiose order. Grand unification doesn't exist. What's the ultimate equation for a huge cauldron of soup? There isn't one! It's just a bunch of broth and carrots and hunks of meat. The same is true of the universe. There's no invisible men or women in the clouds."

"But there's a city council that controls the city."

"Most of it, yes."

"Who are they?"

"I don't know, but I can look their names up in the record books. I can call their offices. I can touch them."

"So what?"

"So they exist to my five senses."

"And anything that doesn't?"

"Doesn't exist. It's the extension of our imagination, designed to comfort us."

"So there's no such thing as happiness?"

She narrowed her eyes. "Touché. But of course there are emotions. There is love. There are feelings we have that instruct our actions. What there is *not*, is an order that assigns us those emotions. There is chaos, there is history, and there is social pressure. But no energies running through us, no auras, no destiny assigned by the cosmos."

"Suppose we use that as a shorthand for chaos, for history, for social pressure," I said. "Add them up and you've got this *thing* — call it what you want."

"I'll call it each of the constituent parts, because they exist. Auras don't. The age of Aquarius doesn't."

"But suppose there's an emergent quality to this *thing*. It's greater than the sum of its parts. Happens all the time. Can't we say that *that's* the divine? The part we can't explain: *That's* the will of the universe."

"It's an artificial explanation for something that doesn't have one."

"Suppose there is an explanation, and we just don't know it yet."

"Fine, then it's a substitute for the truth until we figure it out. Cavemen invented scary monsters to explain thunder."

"And didn't it serve some purpose?"

"Sure. It let the smarter cavemen lead the dumber ones around by the nose."

"But I'm not talking about following some external mandate. I'm talking individualized existence and its teachings for wisdom. Getting into the big picture. So what if people in 4629 decide the emergent quality is the result of a mistake in our math? All I can deal with is what I have here, now. Just like you said. So I call the emergent quality God. What skin is it off your back?"

"Because if you drive over a cat, you'll say it was the fault of the emergent quality."

"No, I'll say I wasn't watching where I was going."

"Most people won't."

"I'm not talking about most people. I'm talking about me."

"Look, you want to convince yourself that anything we can't explain is Divine, you go ahead. But don't believe it means that's *why* those kids in Littleton got killed. The only reason we start these debates is to reassure ourselves when tragedy comes. 'Why do bad things happen to good people?' What a joke! Like being good is supposed to provide immunity to tragedy. It happens. Deal with it. It has always happened, and it will always happen. So just prepare for it, and help others do the same. And be there for others to whom it has already happened. Because if you ask 'why' and don't get the answer you want, *then* what will you do?"

"That's so cold."

"No, it's not!" She was screaming. "That's burning love, brewed from the depths of my soul! It's the love that came to me from my friends when my father died! It's the love that I got from my family when my friend Jonathan died! It's the love that I got when I broke my leg. It's real, it's immediate. It comes when we need it, and we should be ready with it when it's needed. Not only if the person's 'good' or looks like us or he's a guy or if he's heterosexual or lives in a 'normal' community. It's unconditional love. It's grounded in the undiminished understanding that this love benefits the giver as well as the receiver, but it's not selfish, and it's not designed to feed that urge. It says that misery and pain and tragedy and death are inevitable and unavoidable, so we'd better prepare to meet them head-on. Right now. This second. What would you say to me if the reaper suddenly appeared beside you?"

I stammered. I couldn't think of what to say.

"What would you say?"

"I don't—"

"You'd say he was greater than the sum of his parts."

"So is there any way to answer the question, 'Why am I here?'" I asked.

"Because," she said. "On any other planet you wouldn't stand a chance."

"No, I mean here. In this skin."

"Because your parents had sex."

"No, I mean—"

"You mean why are you in the position you're in? Why do you have the resources you do? Why are you human and not a dog? What's your divine purpose? What part of The Plan do you play? Look, you have a purpose on Earth only so long as you believe there's an order to the universe."

"There may not be one in the universe, but there's one on the planet."

"Oh, yeah? Who's in charge of it?"

"The IMF, the World Bank, the WTO, the UN, the CIA, McDonald's, Kodak, Wal-Mart, McDonnell-Douglas, GE. . . ."

She chuckled. "In that order? Okay, so you're here to work. Sell your mind for eight hours a day. Providing the labor laws don't slip anymore."

"But there are alternative world orders being established. Like you said, there are other ways the world could be."

"What, you're gonna go join Hezbollah?"

"No, I'll join the Labor Party. Or an intentional community."

"Have fun. Write when you get work."

"Are you saying they're not viable alternatives?"

"You started out asking me what your purpose was. Is. You seem to have a pretty good idea already."

"I have some ideas, but no definite sense."

"What, you want some giant in a green robe to tell you what the future holds?"

"Look, we have to connect ourselves with something bigger than ourselves, something larger than just our lives. We belong to traditions."

Imposition

"So belong to a tradition. What do you need me for?"

"So let's say I create an amalgam of the people in the tradition to which I believe I belong. Call it a godhead, call it what you want. It's not perfect, it just represents the things those people stood for."

"But sometimes they stand for different things."

"Fine, then — say it's the best of those things."

"Ah ha. And how does this amalgam differ from you?"

"It's not me. It's everything I shoot for."

"A future you."

"A potential me."

"Fine. What's the problem?"

"I'm not like most of them. There are some here and there than I can identify with, but most of them are steeped in other histories."

"There are no other histories. Things happen, whether we remember them or not, and regardless of whether or not our ancestors were there. They still happen."

"But they don't have the same impact as things that are directly tied to us."

"Granted," she said. "We're back to chaos. Small wind, small storm. Big wind, big storm."

"But a small wind can cause a big storm," I said. "That's the truth behind chaos."

"No," she said. "A small wind can *contribute* to a big storm. It's sheer chutzpah to say you're going to *cause* a big storm. Even big winds are only contributing. It's too mixed up. We're all just butterflies. Some are bigger than others, but in the end we're all just the same creatures beating our delicate wings."

"Some of us have bigger wings."

"Yes, thanks to luck, hard work, and — in many cases — piles of corpses. But if you stop there you're an

173

idiot. Yeah, power is distributed along a certain axis. First you have to decide if you're happy with that setup — where the axis is, how it's designed."

"No, first I have to figure out where I am on that axis."

"No, that comes second. Because individuals can move around on it and the structure won't change."

"But maybe I can direct the resources more effectively if I'm higher up."

"Yeah, maybe. But maybe your individual influence will be insignificant. Maybe it's the whole system that needs washing out. Restructuring."

"It's a crap shoot," I said. "Which way will yield better results? How can I know? Which one do I pick? How can I measure the net result of my work? Am I even doing the right thing? Why am I here?"

"All you can do is trust yourself," she said. "Look at the available evidence, and make an intelligent choice. If you look back and decide you made the wrong one, well, there's nothing you can do. You did the best you could."

"I can't stand feeling that way."

"Yeah, but most people probably do. You always feel like you can do more. Get more done. Save more lives, if that's what you're trying to do. Whatever — just do what you can and be happy with your efforts. Concentrate less on the results (like you said, you can't really measure them anyway) and focus on your effort. What did *you* do?"

"But that's just a way of getting out of effective work. 'Oh, I'm doing my best, so it doesn't matter if nothing comes of it.' Gack."

"Not at all. Be open to reflection and criticism, of course. Listen to what your conscience and other people tell you about results. Do what you think will do the most good. But in the end, the only one you have to answer to is yourself."

"And the tradition."

"Why does the tradition need to pass judgment on us?" she asked.

"Because," I said. "It's a legacy that you have to *work* to be a part of."

"But I thought the question was one of your own self-conception. So the only test of whether you're a part of that tradition is: Do you consider yourself to be a part of it?"

"Well, one's self-conception is key, but it's not the only thing. There's an objective examination of the facts that has to take place. I'm not a neurosurgeon just because I say I am. The question is: Does the evidence suggest that I'm skilled in the art of neurosurgery?"

"I'd say it's more of a science," she quipped.

"Ha, ha."

"But you know if you're skilled or not. Whether I believe you is another matter entirely."

"Yes, but in order for you to believe me, the facts must bear me out. The same is true for my place in the tradition. I can delude myself just fine. The question is not how I see myself vis-à-vis the tradition, but how the tradition sees me in relation to itself."

"And how are you supposed to know that?"

"We come back to the amalgam," I said. "How does this entity view people, and how do I compare with its expectations?"

"So can't you be deluded about the amalgam just as easily as you can about you?"

"Sure I can, but it's not as likely. There are infinite mediating factors that we know about ourselves that allow us to convince ourselves that we're whatever we want to be. We can tell ourselves that we're not really the way others see us because we know so much more that they never see or hear. But the sense we get of history — and historical figures, and therefore the tradition — is finite. There is a closed set of information that we draw from to understand the past. We can choose to ignore or downplay a fact about someone we admire, but it's still a fact."

"So there's a true state that the past can exist in, but not one for the living?"

"Hmm." I thought about this. "No, I'd say it this way: We can work only from what is known. For the living, what is known consists of what everyone knows about us, combined with what we know about ourselves. For the dead, it's only a matter of what's known about them, combined with their documentation of what they know about themselves. The key to being honest about your idols (and heroes) is being able to incorporate everything that's known about them into your conception of them as people. And this goes for your relationship to them, too. Can your vision of this person include *everything* you know about them? If not, then your understanding of them is wrong.

"The same is true about history and society," I continued. "If you run into a situation or an event that is inconvenient for your worldview, or just doesn't fit, your worldview may be obsolete. It could be completely, one hundred percent wrong."

"Or it might just be slightly off."

"Yes, but consider physics. If one apple, or one aspirin, or one piece of paper — anything — ever fell upward, it would mean that the theory of gravity is completely wrong. It would blow it all to hell."

"But that's what the theory of relativity did," she said. "Only it didn't blow it all to hell, it encompassed Newton; it engulfed the theory of gravity. It said: 'That's kind of how it works, and that holds true under most circumstances, but it's really just a subset of this theory.' It was more a modification."

"Fine. But my point is that if the initial assumptions are flawed, then the final outcome is likely to be wrong. Not likely — it *will* be wrong. It's just a matter of how long it takes to become apparent. So when we come to an inconvenient fact, the first question should always be: 'Could my framework of assumptions be wrong?' And the the answer should be — it always *has* to be — yes. You always have to be willing to admit that everything you know and believe is wrong. That's the *essence* of having an open mind. If you're not willing to admit that, you're just pretending to have an open mind. And really mean it — we can tell each other all day that our minds are open. Only the person himself knows how true that is."

"So anyway. . . ."

"So anyway, that's the test of a comprehensive framework of assumptions, of a sensible worldview. The answer is not to disavow any sense of large-scale understanding, but rather to maintain one that is flexible. One that is always able to change and readjust. Not that it should just flex in the wind and point whichever way the wind is blowing. But rather open itself up for all perspectives and try to embody diverse opinion and fact, even that with which you might disagree. Only then does the world make sense."

"No," she said. "It doesn't make sense. It only seems like it. We can find evidence to support our conceptions, but then — bam! — along comes some new bit of evidence that shoots it all to hell. What do you do? Most people just ignore the new evidence. So here comes another one — bam! And if it fits, you're vindicated. And if not, you ignore that one too. And so on, until you convince yourself the planet is six thousand years old, and angels are flying around downtown."

"And there's no middle of the road between being suckered in like that and total atheism?" I asked.

"Not one that makes any sense. What, you're going to believe that there's an order in the universe, but it's subject to laws of rationality and logic?"

"Okay, let's take your athiest view. Suppose something makes me step out of the street moments before a bus comes whizzing by. What do I attribute my good luck to? A neuron in my brain firing at just the right time? Or a gust of wind?"

"Why not attribute it to good luck? What's wrong with being lucky? Being lucky makes more sense than believing there's a guardian angel watching over you. Or whatever you call it. Besides, angels only emerge from positive experiences. So where's your angel while you're getting mugged?"

"She's keeping me from getting killed," I said.

"Oh god," she said. "Okay, fine. Let's try the opposite. Let's posit the existence of goblins. Because these angels are supposedly bringing the world to a stable good state — heaven on Earth and all that. Well, the goblins are bringing it to a stable bad state. How about that? So while you're getting mugged, your guardian goblin is introducing your girlfriend to someone incredibly witty and sexy whom she'll eventually dump you for. You're making a decision which one you believe in — angels or goblins. And they're all just imaginary friends."

"But that can help!" I insisted. "It can be comforting to embody chaos like that, to put a face on the universe. Who wants to feel like they're just wandering around in the dark, just randomly having good things or bad things happen to them?"

"Look," she said. "There's nothing inherently wrong with imaginary friends. I respect someone who believes in imaginary friends much more than these angel freaks that you meet all the time. Why? Because an imaginary friend isn't perfect, and they're not sent down from heaven by

God. They're imperfect. They're capable of making mistakes."

"But angels aren't perfect." I paused. "Okay, some people say they are. But most people like 'em just because they're on our side. They're in our corner. And in a world where it's easy to feel like not many people are, that has some value."

"Sure. It lets us ignore our commonality as people and focus on invisible things perched on our shoulders."

"But suppose you don't feel that commonality."

"Lots of people don't," she agreed. "There aren't too many preachers out spreading the gospel of human similarity."

"It's not a very comforting gospel," I said, "when you look around at all the bad stuff happening."

"Maybe not," she said. "But it's the only thing that'll make things better in the long run."

"So without a god, how do we get morality?"

"Well, you're assuming that gods bring morality with them. And they do, to an extent. Each god gives you a set of morals to live by — but each one is different. What makes the morality of Christianity more moral than that of Judaism? Or Hinduism? If there are more Christians, does that make their religion 'correct?' Because they killed more heathens? Is the gospel a selfish gene? Or is Christianity correct because its text is older than the text of another religion? And how do other religions come about if there's one True God? Let's say we adopt the Islamic line and assume that Allah is the one true god. So if I have a religious experience that isn't congruent with Islam's teaching, does that mean that Allah appeared to me, and I misunderstood his message, or that I'm delusional, and only *thought* I saw Allah?

"Now, if you mean to sidestep this discussion (which is a mistake, in my opinion), we can talk about personal conceptions of god. But how do we craft one of those? What's to keep us from sculpting one that happens to approve of whatever we're doing? The point is: With or without a god, our morality comes from our parents."

"What about orphans? Or children of neglectful parents?"

"Well, let me backtrack," she said. "There are millions of influences trying to get to us all the time. Parents decide, at the most crucial time, which influences will have access to us. If they're not around, then other people take on the role — other relatives, social workers, foster parents, nuns, what have you. Teachers play a major role, too. The point is that what we see while we're first figuring out the world forms the foundation from which we go out and interpret the rest of our lives. Other experiences may allow us to compliment that foundation, or even change it completely, but the elements of our value system are formed in childhood and adolescence."

"But a lot of kids rebel against the way they're raised."

"Well, not completely."

"Sure they do."

"No, not really. Not too many kids decide that cannibalism is the way to go."

"Because they'd go to jail."

"That's part of it, but it probably has more to do with the value of human life — however subjective and/or fleeting — that they learn in the early years."

"Okay. So most of our morality comes from mom and dad."

"Or mom and mom; or dad and dad; or Uncle Freddie and Aunt Hill."

"Yeah, yeah. But if *they're* not coming from a divinely-inspired set of morals, what are they using?"

"Well, the church is just one source they have for teaching kids about right and wrong. TV is another. Of course there are lots of different TV shows, but most of it's just mindless entertainment. So kids learn how to be mindless. Then there's the market — and this probably has more influence than TV and movies and music combined. But it's never part of the equation."

"What do you mean?" I asked.

"There's no question that the market has its own values and its own morality that it requires of its participants."

"Values like?"

"Like only the bottom line matters. Like get ahead by any means necessary. Like eat or be eaten. These are things we *live*. We might never say them explicitly, but they are the rules of the game. We may hear about how important it is to be good or else we'll go to hell. But if your job — meaning food for your kids — requires you to pay workers in Indonesia four dollars a day, then that goodness becomes a lot less relevant. And the same thing is more or less true of crack dealers.

"But the market is a human fiction," she said, "just like any other. We could be living in a completely different structure if we wanted."

"Are you a communist?" I asked.

"No," she said. "This isn't about what I am or am not, what I prefer or don't. Maybe I like capitalism. The point is that capitalism has consequences and *requires* a certain belief structure. And belief structures reproduce through indoctrination. So maybe I spoke too soon when I said the market is stronger than radio and TV and movies. It's strong partly because it works *through* those mediums, and in such a way that we don't even notice it! When was the last movie you saw that mentioned capitalism, good or bad? It's a nearly invisible way of replicating itself, indoctrinating us without our knowledge."

"Not all belief structures have to use indoctrination," I said. "Really good ones can survive on open discussion and debate."

"Yeah, but they'll have to defend themselves eventually, because the other belief structures are going to try to silence it, if they can."

"But there will always be rational people who can keep the rational belief structure alive."

"Unless they're all killed."

I sighed a long, uneven sigh. I looked up; it was dark now. "So," I said. "I guess it all comes down to love."

She scratched her head. "Well, yes and no," she said.

"What do you mean, yes and no?"

"Okay. There's no question that love is going to be the salvation of our civilization, if ever there will be one. But at the same time, we shouldn't think of it as a panacea. It's not a cure-all. There are some things that love alone won't fix. If I—"

"Well, of course it's not just a matter of love," I said. "What I'm talking about is a suffusing of love into our consciousness. It's not a cure-all, but without it, everything else is doomed to failure."

"Yes, but here we have to be careful with what we mean when we say 'love.' There's love between men and women, romantic love."

"Or women and women, or men and men."

"Of course. That's not what we need. There's plenty of that in the world already. We're overflowing with that kind of love. What's needed is love for all humanity. Everyone loves their mother. Most people love their spouses, their kids. But who loves — I mean, really *loves* — their next door neighbor? Or more importantly, who loves the people across the tracks, who have less in common with them than their neighbors do? Or the people in the next town? Or in another state? Or another country? It's easy to love the people we live around, but—"

"No it isn't," I said. "It's hard as hell to love the people we live around. I used to hate the guy in the apartment next to mine. He was a scumbag."

"Right. So the question is: Who loves scumbags?" She smiled, but went on. "Seriously. Who loves that guy? And what possible reason could there be for loving him? Maybe your religion guilts you into liking him — love your neighbor, blah blah blah. And maybe there's an internal motivation. Wanting to feel good about yourself and all that crap. But suppose you don't feel that way. Maybe you don't take your religion too seriously. Suppose you'd rather take the path of least resistance and ignore him. Or suppose you get a thrill (maybe one of few in your life) by provoking him. What's the benefit from love in that situation?"

"Because. It's the golden rule. Do unto others—"

"Yeah. But again, you're only doing it because you hope to get the same treatment from him. Suppose, then, that you felt absolutely certain that, despite all the love you show a person, he'll always treat you like garbage. Does it make sense to even bother?"

"Sure it does."

"Why?" she asked.

I hesitated. For a while.

"It does have to do with reaping and sowing," she said finally. "But it requires a more complex picture. It can't just be a matter of doing the right thing — of loving others — because you want it for yourself. It has to be because you want it for *everybody*. Say you're dealing with this guy and you're one hundred percent nasty to him (because you know he's going to be nasty to you, and you figure there's no point in going out of your way to be nice). He takes that negativity and feeds off it; it's the stuff of his day. And he's probably used to that. So he's nasty to someone else, and they're nasty to the bus driver, and the bus driver is nasty to a woman on the bus, and she's nasty to the mailman, and he's nasty to his kids.

"But suppose you're only 90% nasty. We're at the sliding doors now, the butterfly flapping its wings. Maybe that lower degree of nastiness produces the same feeling in him. But maybe it means he's just a little less nasty to the other person. And they're a little nicer to the bus driver, and maybe the woman is at a state where your 100% negative attitude — filtered through all those people — is enough to piss her off, but where she's able to laugh off a 90% level of nastiness. The question is not only how does the world make you feel, but also: As a member of the world, how do you want to make others feel?"

"Sure I'm a member, but just one of six billion."

"Well, you're screaming in the wind, no doubt. But the whisper that comes out can have an effect. The butterfly in New York doesn't *cause* the tornado in Japan, but she contributes to it. And depending on the conditions in the system, the beating of her wings may be the straw that breaks the camel's back. Some people call it the 'toppler' — that last link in a chain of events that causes a big change in the system. The tiny little bit that's needed for the tornado to develop. That's the power of our language. That's the real power we have over each other. Sometimes it's totally insignificant. But sometimes it's the toppler.

"And this goes for everything in the world," she continued. "The amount of love in society, political change, environmental preservation, whatever."

"If I recycle one piece of paper, it'll save one tree."

"Or maybe the demand that your piece of paper satisfies could have been needed to clear-cut a forest."

"It's pointless to think that way," I said. "Besides, the powers that be have more clout than us common folk.

A rich butterfly that can afford to buy a big wind-producing machine can bring about more tornadoes in Japan than a butterfly without one. And if the other butterflies don't want a storm, what can they do?"

"Right," she replied. "But if three thousand butterflies all beat their wings at the same time, maybe they can cancel the machine out."

"Probably not."

"Okay, maybe not. But let's say the rich butterfly with his windmaking machine provides 6,000 units of wind, and a storm brewing in Japan only needs 3,000 units to become a tornado. So maybe the other butterflies can't equal his 6,000 units, but if they create 3,500 units, that's enough to stop the tornado from happening."

"Yeah," I said. "But there's probably another butterfly with another machine pumping out 3,000 more units of his own somewhere else."

"Fine," she said. "So long as there's another group of butterflies flapping together to keep it from mattering. Usually it doesn't work, because money talks and power concedes nothing without a demand. But on the other hand almost all of the good things that we take for granted — the weekend, for instance — are there because a lot of butterflies were flapping their wings at the same time. They might not look alike, these butterflies, and they probably don't agree on everything, or even most things. Or maybe they don't agree on anything else. But in that instance, they got together and flapped their wings in that certain way, and stopped the tornado from happening. And we get to sleep in on Saturday and Sunday as a result. The machines are turned down for a while. But eventually they'll get turned on again. And then the rest of us have to start flapping again. It never stops. But the flapping has an effect."

"Yeah, okay. But in keeping with the idea of different perspectives, shouldn't we be thinking about a whole new system, where the rich butterfly doesn't have such an unfair advantage? Where the machine doesn't exist at all?"

"Go ahead. Lemme know how far you get."

"I might get nowhere. But that doesn't mean it's not the right way to act. The most likely outcome isn't always the best one, or the one we should shoot for. In fact, most of the time the best one is probably the least possible. Or maybe it's almost impossible. Doesn't mean it's wrong. Sometimes we have to reach for the impossible."

"Sure," she said. "But if you do that long enough, and never get what you're reaching for, you'll burn yourself out. Achieving a victory has other ramifications aside from the fact of the victory itself. It's an inspiration to other folks moving in the same direction. It's a motivating factor for those who aren't involved."

"So we should choose tiny, easily achieved goals, so as to feel good about our progress."

"Well, but that's not progress. It's just lots of tiny bits of movement. The key is finding a balance between aiming high and keeping one's feet on the ground. Neither too far nor not far enough shall ye go."

"Well, who's to say which is which?"

"It's a personal question."

"And one for the tradition," I said.

"Sure, fine. But then there's another question. I guess it's related, in a way. It's about adhering to principles, and fine-tuning our actions in accordance to them. Nonviolence is a good example. You can aim for a total overthrow of the ruling class, and maybe you'll get violent Spartacists looking to do the same thing. That's a lofty goal, and you're both seeking it out, but if you believe nonviolence is a prerequisite for any revolution you'll be involved in, you have to make that clear. A revolution isn't a revolution unless the modes of power are changed. Not just a rearrangement of who's on top of the system."

"So you're saying that a violent revolution isn't really a revolution."

"It might be," she said. "But it probably won't be, since violence breeds violence, and those who win the war will have to use the same kinds of force and coersion that were used by the old ruling class. It's just a swap of people, not a change in the way the system works. Either way, that was just an example. What I mean is that without principles behind them, a person's goals can be used to justify any means they require."

"So where do those principles come from?"

"Didn't we already cover this? They develop from the context we live in. So mostly parents, but also the culture at large, what the institutions around us do, and so on. We human beings are incredibly adaptive creatures — we learn how to survive in the midst of whatever situations we find ourselves in. So we're molded by the people around us."

"Society's to blame."

"Yeah, it is. But since we're all members in society — and have the ability, however small, to modify it and contribute to its influence — we're to blame, too. Or, if we're working against the evil and counteracting it with something good, then we're to be commended. Each person reflects society and the way they've been treated, but they also direct: they determine what other people will reflect. We can't decide how other people will act, but we can decide what role we'll play in their lives. What they get from us. And that can matter."

"So is violence ever justified?"
"Is it?"
"I'm asking you."

She smiled. "Well, that may not be the right question. Or at least it's not the first one we should ask."

"Why not? You just went on and on about principles. Well, what about principled violence?"

"But when you start talking about justified violence, it becomes very easy to suit that justification for your own purposes. Find someone who believes there are some instances where violence is justified, and chances are they're the exact instances where he would like to use violence. So that's not the best place to start."

"So where do we start?"

"The real question is: Where does violence come from? Why do people use violence?"

I shrugged. "Because they don't see another alternative."

She nodded. "In some cases, yes. But again, it's easier to pick up a gun and claim there's no alternative than it is to really explore and investigate — and make use of — those alternatives. The other question is: Whose violence are we talking about? A woman who kills her abusive husband is using a very different kind of violence than her husband."

"No she isn't. She's just using it for different reasons. It has the same effect."

"Well, not really. An abusive husband is violent in order to get control and power. He seeks to conquer, to make the woman submissive and to enslave her to him. But when she uses violence in response, she's seeking freedom from that enslavement. And the same is true of slave revolts, anticolonial uprisings, what have you."

"But they're all struggles for power," I said. "They're all looking for control."

"Right. But the dominant forces — battering husbands, oppressive governments, gaybashers — want control over other people. Those fighting back — abused women, colonized people — want control over themselves. And here we come back to the question of a revolution. It can happen that a group fighting for control over itself finds itself fighting for control over other people. Priorities shift, and balances of power change. So the true goal of a revolution, again, is not a new regime that exercises power over the people, but for the people to have power over themselves. Over their own lives. And this requires a different kind of violence, if we can say it's required. So that's one question.

"Now then," she continued, "you mentioned power, and that's really key here. But power doesn't exist all by itself. First of all, it's constantly changing. Those with power now haven't always had what they have. At times they've had less, at times more. And with this constant change comes fear. If you've got power, you're always worried someone's going to try and take it. Shakespeare was right — there's no more worried head than the one that wears the crown."

"Except that nowadays there's not much power in the crown."

"Sure. So the Queen of England isn't worried about folks trying to take the throne. Instead, she's got the same worries as the non-royal rich people: CEOs and the upper one percent. Car alarms, home security systems, gated communities. Walled off, even! There's nothing they fear more than someone coming to take their stuff. And the scary thing is that this leads them to support policies that leave innocent people dead.

"Let's say a black man is found walking around in one of these communities at night. The police approach him and for some reason he doesn't immediately lie down. They shoot him, because they assume immediately that he's there to swipe their merchandise. And the police are acquitted, because the mandate from the people in charge is clear: None of 'those people' are allowed in this part of town without a gardener's uniform. This paranoid fantasy of members of the underclass coming to loot and pillage is the driving force behind city planning and architecture these days."

"But it's not their stuff that people really want," I said. "It's power."

"Sure. But it's a lot easier to grab a rich man's BMW than it is to grab his decision-making power. Or his tax cut lobby. Or his corporate assets. But again, that's because there are all kinds of things keeping *that* from happening. Union busting, government counterinsurgency, political imprisonment and assassinations. You try to fight the power — really fight the power at the top — and you'll face a backlash. That's totally natural, that's how it works. And it's because of fear. Those with power are afraid of those who want to take it.

"And this is also true on a smaller scale. So say in a ghetto, someone with more money is going to be very worried about getting robbed."

"And that's a real fear, because people in a ghetto are more desperate for money."

"Right. Now, I've never lived in a ghetto, so this is all speculation. But of course people in the suburbs aren't scared of their neighbors, for the most part. They're scared of the people on the other side of the tracks. But those on the other side of the tracks are scared of each other. Put six rabbits in a tiny cage with one carrot, and see what happens. The same rabbits act very differently than they would if they were in seperate cages. Now, I don't want to reduce the complexities of human existence to simplistic rabbit analogies, but it's a framework for the discussion. And I think it's safe to say it's not too far from reality. Twenty years ago, a song called 'The Message' came out. The lyrics said: 'It's like a jungle sometimes / it makes me wonder how I keep from going under.' Sort of the same thing we've got here.

"The folks in the suburbs benefit from keeping the rabbits in their cages. Get them to fight with each other, to steal each other's stuff, and they'll leave you alone. It's a pretty simple case of divide and conquer. If they're busy burning Compton, they'll stay away from Simi Valley. If they're mad at the Asians who own the corner store, that takes attention away from the white CEOs of the banks, who are really calling the shots. The reality of the ghetto is not an accident, whether it's a ghetto in Krakow in 1935 or a ghetto in Los Angeles in 1995. It's not a natural course of events. And it's certainly not due to laziness or low morals among the people in the ghetto. The cages are real, they come from decisions that are made by people on the outside, and those decisions have intentional consequences."

I nodded. "But the people in the suburbs are in cages, too."

"Right," she said. "And that's the final irony. This system leaves everyone in a kind of prison. Of course, the conditions in the suburban cages are a lot nicer than those in the ghetto. But they're still cages. There's a lot of fear, a lot of confusion, a lot of rage in those suburban cages. So if you're a kid caught up in all of this, without a firm grasp on dealing with that confusion and rage, maybe you find some guns and shoot up Columbine High School. Or look at that day trader in Atlanta a few months back who went nuts and killed his family and all those people in his 'office'. He was under such immense pressure from the economic system, which is aligning against working folks, and eroding the structures of support like community organizations and unions. But look at what happened in the media after that happened. There was a brief discussion about how day trading is risky and unstable, but most of the news was about how crazy this guy was and how random the incident was.

"In Columbine, all we heard for two solid weeks was about how horrible the video games are, and how the music made these kids into killers, and how the Internet taught them to murder. But in Atlanta, the very obvious economic pressures that drove this man to the brink of insanity got almost no scrutiny. There was no mention in the media about how the whole *system* is like that, even though we all know it. Everyone's worried about the future. Everyone knows that the stock market could crash any day now. Everyone's in debt. Everyone's struggling to keep their heads above water. Everyone's looking for something to cling to. Everyone's in cages. But we're convinced that our illusions are less painful than reality.

"What we need is not a system of different people in different cages, like Stalinism or some other state-controlled structure. What we need is a system without cages. And it's not impossible. We can do it. But we have to start by considering what we want. Even if it's something that's never happened before doesn't mean it never will. Do you think abolitionists thought slavery would always exist in the U.S. because it always had? Because some form of slavery has been a mainstay of human existence for all of history? No. If it's wrong, it's wrong, and we can do better. And we're back to the question of the supreme order. We're told that the order we've got is the only one possible. That it's an order ordained by nature. But that's bollocks, because there *is* no order that's ordained by nature. Slavery was said to be ordained by nature — not to mention the Bible and the Constitution. But that was all smoke and mirrors. The same is true today."

"But those with power aren't going to give it up without a fight," I said. "So how do we make that change without violence?"

"Maybe we can't," she said solemnly. "Is violence justified in that case, considering the counterviolence it'll

Imposition

cause? I don't know if I can say. And there's a larger issue. Even if the counterviolence dies down, what we end up with is a system that is still based on coercion and force. It's not a system of free association.

"If I take your candy bar, and you beat me up and take it back, you have your candy bar back, but there's no guarantee I won't try to get it again. Or try and steal the next bar you get. I'm always going to want what you have, despite the force you use to make sure I don't get it. So the question is: Why do I want it in the first place? Why don't I have a candy bar of my own? And that's where history comes in. Maybe it's my own fault I don't have a candy bar. Maybe not. Either way, the real tragedy is that under our current structures, the question doesn't even get asked.

"But let's even say it *is* my own fault that I don't have a candy bar. Suppose you decide to share some of your candy bar with me anyway."

"Then I'm a sucker," I said.

"Maybe," she replied. "Or maybe you're demonstrating that we don't have to live in a world based on a philosophy of 'Keep your hands off my stuff or I'll kill you.' Maybe you're showing me that there's another way."

"And maybe you'll just take me for all I'm worth."

She nodded. "Yeah, maybe. But maybe I'll realize — especially if it happens over and over again — what's really going on. Unless a person's mentally unstable or refuses to use their brain, they're going to start thinking about what's happening and consider their role in it. Maybe we'll both be changed by the experience. Maybe the next time around, when I have a candy bar and you don't, I'll be more likely to share it with you.

"Maybe violence is needed in some cases. But maybe it's only a quick fix that really doesn't solve anything. There are other ways of making change, ways that aren't based on force or coercion. And the real question, then, is whether or not these methods are effective enough to bring about enough change to quell the desire for quick fixes. Or do the conditions brought about by a quick fix justify the methods used? Violence may seem necessary at times, but is it ever justified?"

"Is it?"

"I'm asking you."

I smiled.

"Is there any way to establish a third option?" I asked. "Between dogmatic religious fanaticism and total withdrawal from questions of spirituality? Can you make a leap of faith and stay grounded in reality?"

She chuckled. "Only if you're willing to strand yourself over a chasm of uncertainty. If your feet are on the ground, but you're reaching for god, your midsection is hovering over an abyss."

"Yeah, but that's true for everyone. I mean, athiesm isn't a guarantee, either. You agree that there's such a thing as happiness."

"But it's more of a stretch to believe in a god. There's more uncertain ground to cover."

"Fine. But suppose we develop a kind of scientific faith, one based not on ancient books or hallucinations or orders barked at us in a special building once a week, but on our own experience with a living divine presence."

"What do you mean?"

"Let's say I stay up really late one night writing," I said. "Because I can't sleep. Even though I have to get up early the next day."

"Okay. So?"

"Let's say the reason I can't sleep is because I drank a lot of coffee that evening and it's keeping me awake. Doesn't it make sense to say that there's something about the story that needs to get itself written? That this is compelling me to work on it?"

"Don't be ridiculous," she said. "*You* decided to drink the coffee."

"Yes, I did."

"Well, why did you make that choice?"

"For a number of reasons. I was hanging out in a coffee shop with friends. But part of it was because I wanted to be awake and enjoy the evening."

"So how does this have anything to do with what you're writing?"

"Because!" I exclaimed. "Once I leave the coffee shop and go home and check my email and watch some TV and get ready for bed, I'm still wide awake and have no choice but to break out the pen and paper and have at it."

"Is there something especially compelling about the subject you're writing on?"

"Yes, but that's only one factor out of many. And that's the point. The order emerges when we're able to recognize so many factors pointing in a certain direction, seemingly without any coordination. The order we create — or recognize, depending on your point of view — is an acknowledgment of that pattern, combined with a hypothesis about where it's going, with a touch of our own hopes and desires thrown in. *That's* the divine. That's how we relate to the universe rationally and spiritually at the same time. The chasm we're stretched across isn't empty, it's filled with elements from both sides of the leap. Where they meet is the river of belief. It's not fact, but it's not fake either. It's kind of in-between. A sort of quantum wellspring of reality. It's where happiness comes from. It's a turbulent mixture of tangible evidence and . . . something else.

"Look at cognitive psychology. Look at neurochemical evolution. Look at the consumer price index. Look at cycles of culture. In every case, you find patterns and motion, melody among dissonance. And sometimes what looks like dissonance is really melody."

"And vice versa," she said.

"Absolutely!" I replied. "Simplicity that looks like complexity, and vice versa. Chaotic patterns and patterned chaos. Maybe it's all accidental. It *could* be, we agree on that. But maybe it isn't. At this point we have about as much proof for one as for the other. And this isn't Chicken Little — we all know the sky isn't falling."

"Most of us, anyway."

"Right. But at the same time, *something* caused the Big Bang. *Something* allowed life to exist on land. *Something* or some*things* pushed me to write that night. A mystery of science is a form of spiritual quandary: How are you going to approach it? Religions tell us only to see those facts that fit the mold. But the scientific, athiestic response breaks everything into quarks and electrons. But with the patterns we've begun to see, the divine force driving our perception is the ability to step back and look at it another way. These days it's not a matter of not being able to see the forest for the trees; we can't see the trees for the microscopic bark and leaf scrapings. So what *is* a tree? In how many ways does it exist, and which ways mean the most to people and why? And what does a tree mean to you?

"A conception of the universe that allows us to see trees as nothing but potential telephone poles is doomed to self-destruct. So is one that sees them as nothing but quarks and electrons. So is one that sees them as nothing but a place to sit while writing poems. So is one that sees them as nothing but reincarnated dead people."

"So you're talking about a theory of everything," she said.

"No," I said. "More like a set of theories of all things. Not one tool that does it all, but a group of tools to achieve perspectives uncommon to the standard gaze. There is no one way, no single answer. If you think there is, you're wrong. Multiplicity is key. Trying to essentialize all the universe into one idea is a dead end. The magic formula — the true theory of everything — is a *complete* understanding of how all those conceptions work with one another, and compete with one another."

"But that's impossible."

"Of course it is. So the best we can do is to approximate, look at trends and patterns, and switch perspectives often. Only by constantly looking at the box we're in, and moving outside it, can we reach any sort of harmony with ourselves. If you ever stop trying to learn 'why?' you might as well be dead."

She nodded. "But even that structure can be used to suit one's needs. If you notice a pattern leading to something good, that's the presence of the divine. You see what you want to see. But if it leads to something bad, what is that?"

"It could also be the presence of the divine," I said. "It's time to lose this idea that the divine is absolutely and only good. The real truth in such a conceptualization is that the divine is everywhere at all times. But it's not really a matter of a pattern being good or bad; the element itself is essentially value-free. The only thing making something divine is its ability to connect things that appear to be disconnected, random. Suppose a pattern is found in a dynamic system, and it points to an undesired outcome (this is about as close as we can come to good versus evil without subscribing to a dogmatic morality). We might freak out and call it the devil's work. But suppose that pattern turns out to be a tiny segment in an even larger pattern. What level of desirability does that larger pattern suit? And what if this larger pattern is part of an even larger one? If we look at it this way, we eventually ask what the largest pattern is, which is akin to asking: What's the mind of the universe? And only the most naive simpleton can really believe that humans will ever know this. So it becomes a matter of faith. What do you think the big picture is a picture *of*?

"And it's not merely a religious question, by the way. Scientists have to decide what level they're going to focus on, and how simple or complex they'll make their questions, and their worldview. And this is a philosophical consideration, with practical implications. But at the higher levels, it's more or less the same question: What is the big picture a picture of?"

"But once you decide that," she said, "you have to fit all your perceptions into that image."

"Or else reconsider the image. In any case, the image shouldn't be a dominating force. It's a backdrop. It's a setting for the smaller pictures; it's a context. It should be flexible, to allow for seemingly arbitrary elements within it. But again, the whole kit and caboodle should be open to change. And it doesn't have to be one thing — it can be multiple things at the same time. And that's the key: To see things from as many directions as possible at once.

"Take you and me, for example. If someone were to walk into this room right now, they wouldn't necessarily know what we have to do with each other. You could be my sister. Or I could be your boyfriend."

She chuckled. "Or both."

I laughed. "Yeah, or both. Or you could be a census taker and I could be a resident. Or we could be roommates. Or we could be cousins. Or complete strangers who happen to be in the room together. Maybe you're married to my roommate's best friend and we're waiting for them to get back from the movies. Maybe your lesbian partner is a CIA spy who's out on assignment and I'm a secret service worker here to protect you. All of these are possible."

"Ah," she said, raising a finger. "But the person walking into the room could do some research and find out what the real relationship between us is."

I nodded. "Yes, but suppose for a moment that we're in a play, and in that play you're my mother. Now since we're about the same age, you'd have to wear makeup and use other tactics to appear to be my mother. But in the context of the play, the relationship between us is mother and son. And people would believe that, if we did it right."

"Yeah, but in reality it's something different, and research would prove that. We're not both things at the same time."

"Yes, but while the relationship between us in 'real life' is one thing, we're also co-stars in real life, in the context of the play. If someone wrote a story about us, we'd be characters in it, while simultaneously sharing whatever other relationship we have. I am my mother's son at the same time that I'm a taxpayer."

She nodded.

"Here's another example," I said. I ripped a piece of blank white paper from the journal and drew a series of dots. I showed it to her. "What is this a picture of?"

"It's a cross," she said.

I nodded, smiling. "Yes, it is. If you connect these dots along the straight lines they're in, you get a cross. Show this to anyone, and they'll tell you it's a picture of a cross. But it's also a bunch of dots. You have to choose to connect the dots in order to see a cross."

"But it's automatic. You can't look at it and *not* see a cross."

"Maybe an alien could," I said. "Or someone raised in a place where Christianity was unknown. Or at least the cross shape. Actually, it's not even a bunch of dots. It's ink on paper. Our mind groups them into dots, recognizing where the ink gathers together. In any case, the scientific view — the rational one, the strictly athiest view — is that this is *only* ink on paper, or if you want to be generous, only a series of dots. In that view, to call it a cross is to see things that aren't there. You say it's a picture of a cross, and that it's impossible *not* to see a cross. And most people would agree. But what is it that makes us think that way?"

"Well, what is a line? It's a bunch of dots. So this is just a spaced out line."

"Right," I said. "So how many dots does it take to make a line?"

"Two."

"Right. You *can* make a line with two dots, but how many dots does it take to *force* you to make a line? If I show you two dots, do you have to make a line out of them? If I show you sixteen dots in a row, is that necessarily a line?"

"It depends on where they are in relation to each other, and how close together they are."

"Ah ha. So we're back to context. Are we allowed to ask that question? Is it a line, or a line segment? Are we allowed to have segments? What rules are we bound by? Are we allowed to see this as something other than a cross?"

"What do you mean?"

I took the paper back and scribbled numbers under the dots. "Now what is it a picture of?"

She traced the path of numbers from 1 to 36 with her finger. "It's a spiral," she said.

"What makes it a spiral?"

"The numbers."

"Right. That's a way of someone else telling you what to see. Let's call that a political view. You're being ordered to look at it as a spiral. But like you said, when you first look at it, it looks like a cross. It still does. If we were to connect the dots according to the numbers, it would be harder to see the cross. Filling in the lines in a certain way kind of closes off the other possibilities, but not completely — it would still be possible to imagine it as a cross. As it is right now, though, it's all three: a cross, a spiral, and a bunch of dots."

"And ink on paper."

"Right. But suppose I see something else."

She stared at the paper.

I waited.

She looked up at me, then back at the paper. Then up at me. "Like what?"

I smiled. "Well, I'm not much of an artist, but let's pick an easy one. What if we connect all the dots on the outer edge? Then the ones inside that circle? And the ones inside that one? Then what do we have?"

"A bunch of concentric circles."

"Well, yeah. Ellipses, really."

"Whatever."

"Or let's connect them this way: Two, three, one, four, ten, eleven. . . ." I pointed to the numbers as I spoke.

"You get a zig-zag."

"Right. But whatever picture I choose to see, it can still be seen as all the other things. And science can call itself the 'real truth,' since all the pictures are just ink on paper. But any moment when something more than ink on paper appears, you're in the presence of the divine. There's no value judgment on the image — it's not good or bad. Maybe it's what you want to see, or maybe it's the last thing in the world you want to see. Those are questions about ideological manipulations of the divine. But the fact that you see anything at all, besides ink on paper, is proof of something beyond the five senses. Something bigger than ourselves. And whether you consider it to be secular, like traditions of people, or religious like a god, the fact is — and I think we've proven that it is a fact — it exists. Maybe we won't ever understand it. Maybe we can't."

"Probably not."

"Probably not. But whether we understand it or not, it's there."

The Fiction Journal
31 Shorties

for my students — past, present, and future

Every day in my Creative Writing class, I put two prompts on the board — one fiction and one non-fiction. Then we write for ten minutes. I have written over a hundred little stories in response to the fiction prompts.

These are a few of my favorites, in no particular order. In most cases they have been tweaked and revised after the initial burst of writing. After each story I've included some notes and the original prompt.

1. The Envelope

Jake threw a fistful of candy wrappers onto the ground. Nino, our cat, pawed over to them and sniffed one, timidly. Jake continued to chuck things out of the brown grocery bag that served as our wastebasket.

From my seat on the couch — where I was watching the news — I could see random debris flying into the air. "Where is it?" Jake demanded, shooing Nino away.

"What are you looking for?" I asked. There was no answer, so I asked again. "What are you looking for?"

"That catalogue I got in the mail from that poster company," he said, exasperated, as if I should know psychically that of course he was looking for a poster catalogue.

"Why?" I said. "I thought you didn't want any of those."

"I don't," he said, hurling some wadded tissues behind him. One of them landed in Nino's water bowl. She fired an icy glare at Jake. "I think I put my paycheck in it and accidentally threw it out. *Where is it?*"

"I gave that catalogue to Susan," I said.

He froze. "What!?"

"You said you didn't want it, so I let her have it. You've seen all the posters in her room."

He dashed to the phone. "What's her number?"

I told him. He dialed.

"Hello, Susan?" He paused. "Oh. Is Susan there? Thanks." Another pause. On TV, Dan Rather spoke in a tired voice about the Florida election mess. I went to the TV to turn it up; the remote had disappeared months ago.

"Hello, Susan? Yeah, this is Jake. No, *Jake*. I'm Mike's roommate. Yeah, you know that catalogue he gave you? Did you look through it yet?" He waited. "*What*? Really? When? When today? So you didn't even glance through it?" More waiting. "No, I know. I know. Yeah, I've seen all the posters in your room." He sighed. "Well, do you remember where you threw it out?" He put a hand to his face and grumbled. "Which Burger Shack? The one on Main Street?" He sighed. "No, yeah, okay. Thanks anyway. Huh? Because I think my paycheck was in it. Yeah, well, I'll find it. Thanks." He dropped the phone and scowled at me. I smiled back.

"I guess I get to root around in the Burger Shack dumpster now," he said. He grabbed his keys and traipsed toward the door.

"Have fun," I said with a grin. He slammed the door behind him, started up his truck, and drove off in a huff.

I got up to turn off the TV. As I glanced behind the set, I noticed a thin white envelope on the ground. I reached over and picked it up. I looked at the phone and thought about calling the Main Street Burger Shack. Then I saw Nino scowling at the tissue in her water bowl and let the envelope fall back to the ground.

The prompt: "Write a story about someone digging through the trash." When I took a second crack at this prompt, I started with the most disgusting descriptions I could imagine. It eventually turned into "Lost Track".

2. Susie the Slug

Susie the slug slithered slowly southward. Sad, she stopped to speculate on the sorry state of her sister Stephanie. Steph's staph infection had suddenly supersized itself on Saturday. By Sunday, the sundry smells and scary symptoms of her sorrowful sickness had swelled and stood out like spots on a sunflower.

Susie's son Simon, standing at Steph's side, silently slipped her a sedative. He saw a spot for sly scavenging, and struck. As Steph sank into sleep, he swiped her sack of sawbucks and split. He scurried swiftly to Switzerland and spent September sipping scotch and soda.

The first sentence is the prompt here. I tell the kids they can continue with mostly s-words ("but not the s-word"), or switch to a different letter with every sentence.

3. The Maybe List

"Listen, man, we've been friends for a long time and I need to tell you something." Luis crouched forward in his chair, his eyes tense with nervous excitement.

I lowered by Deluxe McKangaroo Burger and paused. "Uhh, okay," I said. I had only met Luis the day before, but he seemed like a cool guy. I waited.

He stared at me, his pupils burning with intensity. He hadn't touched his own food yet. It was wrapped tightly, an efficient bundle of assembly-line production. A green +M signaled extra mustard in his milkshake. I kept waiting, but he just kept staring.

I started to feel really uncomfortable. Did he need to borrow money? Maybe he owed, like, thousands of dollars to some crime lord somewhere. Did he have some weird illness? Maybe he only had, like, one month to live. Or maybe he was living some double life, and he couldn't keep it secret anymore. Maybe he was about to tell me what it's like being Bruce Wayne.

I shifted in my seat and set down my Deluxe McKangaroo Burger. I wasn't hungry anymore; my mind was spinning with all the possibilities. Suddenly this guy I thought might be a cool new friend was a major source of stress and might completely screw my life up.

"So," I said, trying to ease him along. "What is it?"

He stared for a few more seconds, took in a deep breath, and let it out real slow. "I'm a spy," he said.

I glanced around, then at his t-shirt with the cartoon football field. "Uhhh," I said. "You don't really look like a spy."

He sat back and let out a mocking breath. "Well who *does* look like a spy, dude? The guy you *think* is a spy is the *last* person you should suspect." He gestured to his head. "Don't you get it, man?"

"I guess not." I picked up my burger and resumed eating. So Luis wasn't a cool guy. I guess he's just a weirdo. I'll keep him on The Maybe List for Future Friends. "So," I said around a mouthful of kangaroo meat, "who are you a spy for?"

"Right now I'm working for the Russian government," he said. "But I'm a freelancer, mostly."

"Right," I said, taking a sip of my soda and rolling my eyes. "And when the Russian government needs a spy, they contact a skinny thirteen-year-old from—" Before I could finish, the place exploded in a barrage of gunfire and flying chairs and three guys came running in, but three other guys appeared from nowhere, shouting Russian profanities, and they all started fighting with switchknives and there were hamburger buns and mustard packets and bottles of vodka flying everywhere and then just as suddenly as it had all begun it was all over, except Luis was muttering something into his wristwatch and two robots came scurrying out of the utility closet and they cleaned up all the mustard and vodka and in thirty seconds they were gone and everything was exactly as it had been.

Luis looked up as he unwrapped his sandwich. "You were saying?"

"Uh," I said. "What just happened?"

He smirked. "What just happened is I just moved from your Maybe List of Future Friends to your List of Most Awesome People You've Ever Met. That's what just happened."

The first line of dialogue is the prompt here. I tell my students to keep their ears open for interesting things people say — cf. Lewis Black's horse/college story. But I'm pretty sure this line came out of a book. I love writing action sequences with run-on sentences like the one at the end there. I think I was trying to mimic Stanislaw Lem's style in <u>Peace on Earth</u>.

4. Mother Kendra

The family was stunned. Grandpa gave us his patented "Don't look at me" look, just like when grandma had announced her plan to learn C++, and then later when she declared her plan to become the next Steve Irwin.

My mother was passing me the mashed potatoes. My dad set the cranberry sauce down and sighed.

"Mom," he said patiently, "c'mon, this is not a good idea. What about your arthritis?"

Grandma took a swig of her malt liquor and gave a "pfff" noise. "That's nothing but some BS limitation Doctor Jablorsky's trying to slap on me. Can't hold *me* back." She raised her right hand and bent her middle and ring fingers inward. One year ago at the previous Thanksgiving, she had explained this as "throwing her set up". But so far as we could tell, this was something she had developed with her bridge club, and the only gang activity she was involved in was playing trump cards while hollering "Yeah, what! Talk some smack now, punk!"

"You could get hurt, Mother Kendra," my mom said, but grandma waved a derisive hand.

"So what?" she said, and pulled her fitted baseball cap down. "You could get hurt driving ninety miles an hour in a school zone, but I still do it."

My five-year-old brother Isaiah had a dazed smile and wide eyes. "I think skydiving sounds cool," he said.

"Yeah, ha?" Grandma said loudly, and took out her earbud. "You wanna come?"

"No *way*," my dad said. "You are *not* taking your five-year-old grandson to go skydiving."

Grandma glared at him and shook her head slowly. "You are such a hater."

Dad rolled his eyes. We ate in silence for several minutes.

Then a low booming noise was not so much heard as felt. We recognized the heavy distorted bass notes a full minute before the noise of the hydraulics on a '63 Cadillac began to flex and pound.

"Op," Grandma said, jumping up. "Estelle's here!" She gave Grandpa a kiss on the cheek and tore the last remaining leg off the turkey. "We're bouncing out to that new club uptown," she said, gnawing on the poultry meat. "So long, suckers!"

She slammed the door behind her and the car squealed off into the night.

For some reason, the kids don't laugh until the line about the school zone. The prompt is: "Gloria's grandmother decides to go skydiving." Fans of The Jerky Boys will recognize Mother Kendra's first rejoinder to the five-year-old.

5. Rorschach's Journal

October 6th: Continued discomfort in the throat today. Illiterate trust fund hippie who calls himself my doctor urged me again to give up my three-pack-a-day unfiltered smoking regimen. I coughed up a thick wad of blood and tar, then grimaced at him and said: "Fine like this." He asked if I might at least remove my face so he could check my nose and ears for infection. When I refused, he offered me a lollipop as a bribe. Intrigued, I asked: "What flavor?" Grape, he said. I just laughed. Then I told him: "I didn't make an appointment to come see you. *You* had an appointment to see *me*." He lunged for me, trying to peel off my face. He said it was for my own good. I jabbed him in the eye with a tongue depressor and escaped through the third-story window. Never compromise. Never surrender.

October 7th: Swine flu continues to assault my throat lining, causing me to talk like hideous demon child. Had to repeat my order to the sniveling rodent at the Burger Shack drive-thru *four* times. As I waited for my food, I watched a half-dead cockroach flail around uselessly in the gutter, its legs pinned by a bloody mass of garbage and filth. Then the wretched acne-scarred idiot at the window handed me a disgusting paper bag filled with greasy food that will clog my arteries and fill my abdomen with parasitic botulism. As he flashed his dead smile through yellowed teeth of pathetic regret, he asked me if I wanted any ketchup packets. And I looked down at him from the window of my truck and whispered: No.

Most fan-fiction is tedious and dreadful. It usually requires an obsessive knowledge of the original text(s), and then its quality is sadly lacking in comparison. When I first came up with this prompt, however — "Write an entry (or two) in the diary or journal of a fictional character" — I *couldn't resist a nod to <u>Watchmen</u>. Reading it with the proper voice in class can be rough. It's fun to hear students familiar with the original catch on.*

6. Bashira in New Vegas

Bashira tilted her hat back and gazed at the valley below. "So this is New Vegas," she said.

Fiery shards of setting sun raked the decimated landscape, rusted signs draped askew on bent poles. She felt the longing of shadows and wondered what might lurk behind the rotting automobile carcasses on the highway.

Suddenly a slug of metal pain shot through her brain as a noisy grunting pounded her ears. "There you are!" the guttural voice bellowed as she collapsed to the ground. She whirled just in time to see some freakish bulging mass of muscle raise his iron club again, screaming painfully. Bashira rolled to the right and pulled the shotgun off her back, pointed it at the monster's grotesque leg, and blasted. It shrieked a bloodcurdling roar — AAURGHH! — and Bashira jumped to her feet.

"Stand still!" the creature wailed. "I'm hungry!" But Bashira did *not* stand still. She dashed around to the monster's left side and leveled the shotgun again, then pulled the trigger and felt her heart freeze when she heard the click.

"No," she gasped. "No no no nonono NO! Not right now!" She chucked the broken weapon to the rocky ground and turned to run, but the beast was upon her and smashed her with the club, breaking her arm.

"Found you!" he screamed, and advanced again, swinging the huge metal bar until a shot cracked the desert air and the mutant howled and gurgled and collapsed beside her.

Bashira looked up from her cringing fetal position and saw a tall man in a dirty Vault 101 jumpsuit crest the hill to the west. "You're lucky I had some VATS energy left," he said, offering his hand. She smiled and let him help her to her feet. "That arm looks bad," he said. "Let's get you to Red over in Big Town."

"I don't have any caps," Bashira said.

"That's okay," the man said. "She owes me a favor."

More fan-fiction. I put the first two sentences up on the day Fallout: New Vegas *came out. I found "Bashira" on an internet list of baby names. It's Swahili, meaning "Predictor of good news". If you're angry because Big Town is near Washington DC and therefore nowhere close to New Vegas, then you're a big nerd. (It so happens that Red started a new Big Town when she moved west.)*

7. A Love Letter from John Rambo to Galadriel the Elf Queen

Hey, hotness, check it out. You're like a total elven hottie. The very first time I came to Rivendell — blasting everything to hell with my huge machine gun and explosive bow-and-arrow set — I was all like "Dude! That Galadriel chick is *hot!*"

Sorry about shooting all those elfs, by the way. I thought I saw an orc in that forest, and as you know, the only way I know of to deal with people that I feel threatened by is shooting them and everything near them. Just be glad I didn't have my claymores with me! :)

Hey, did that midget ever make it to Doom Mountain with the magic bracelet or whatever? Because if you need help with that, I could call my buddy The Rock — he knows a thing or two about Doom. And, like me, he likes to shoot everything around him into submission.

So how's the other elfs? Everything cool in your neck of the woods? Did that one chick get her human boyfriend back? Because if not, maybe I could go and shoot some stuff. (I know it probably won't help, since that situation — like most things in the real world — can't be remedied by shooting big guns. But I figure I'd offer, since I don't have any other way of interacting with people.)

Yeah, so write back soon. I hope you're still hot and we can go on a date sometime, like to the shooting range or something.

John Rambo

The prompt: "Write a letter from one fictional character to another." Because it came out on my birthday one year, I dragged my friends to the Rambo movie where he goes to Burma. The people around us were angry that we were laughing and talking through the movie, but I was angry that people could take such ludicrous snuff-film revenge fantasies seriously. When I read it in class, some kids get the references to <u>Lord of the Rings</u> and some get the Rambo allusions, but the overlap on that venn diagram is miniscule. That's the last fan-fic entry.

8. The Heart of Fair Gwendolyn

"I have just what you need," the old woman said, and ducked into the back room. I stood awkwardly in the bare, dusty shop, glancing nervously at the racks of truth serums and bubbling potions.

Finally, I thought, *Gwendolyn will be mine*. For three years I had tried to win her heart. She was my friend — had been, since we were children — but for some reason she refused my romance advance. I had tried serenading her in the moonlight, filling her bedchamber with sweet roses, even sacrificing a goat and spelling her name with its blood on my face and wearing that around town for a week. Nothing had worked.

Then my friend Simon told me about Old Hag Kelbich's Shoppe of Wondrous Goods, hidden here in the foot of The Chaos Mountains. It had taken three days to get here, and I had lost two of my best sled dogs. But it would all be worth it to win the heart of fair Gwendolyn.

"Ah, yes," the old woman said, emerging from the back room. "With this object, you shall win the heart of any lady you like." She handed it to me.

"A toothbrush!?" I exclaimed.

"Yes," she said, raising a hand to block the air between us. "She doesn't wanna kiss you because you smell like a rat with herpes. Now get your nasty dog crap breath-having diseased mouth-smelling butt out of my shop."

Another line of dialogue prompt. For the record, I have no idea what a rat with herpes smells like.

9. Today Was a Good Day (for Chang)

"Okay," Chang said. "No matter what happens, I'm *going* to have a good day today." He stepped out the front door with a lively bounce in his step. He brushed a speck of dirt off his new cream-colored Def Threads extra baggy deluxe pants. "Fresh," he said with a grin. So preoccupied was he with his new pants that he didn't see the garbage truck drive through the huge puddle on the street. A wave of muddy trash water doused his calves.

"Argh!" he cried, but quickly took a breath. "No," he said. "Gotta stay positive. I'm having a good day." He scratched his nose. "At least I don't have to worry about keeping them clean anymore," he said with a smile, and continued toward school.

As he crested the final hill, he saw his girlfriend Jackie chatting with a group of friends. Then he noticed she was holding hands with a guy he didn't recognize. He marched over to them.

Jackie looked bored. "Oh hey Chang," she said, not bothering to break off from the group. "I think we should see other people or whatever."

Chang froze, scowled, and gestured at the guy holding her hand. He was at least forty years old, wore tattered rag-like clothing, and smelled like a dead sewer rat. "Who the fudge is this?" Chang demanded.

"This is Bob," Jackie said. "He's inbred and he's got a lot of diseases."

Bob coughed violently into his right hand, spewing gobs of phlegm and snot into his palm. Then he extended it to Chang. "Hey man, how's it going?" he asked.

Chang was dumbstruck with disbelief. He gawked at Jackie, unable to find words suitable for the moment. After twenty seconds of awkward silence, Bob brutally cleared his throat and spat on the grass. "Hey man," he said to Chang, "do you have two dollars I could have?"

A pained growl exploded from Chang's chest. He turned and stormed away. "Good day," he said. "Good day." it was low and rocky in his throat. "Good day. Good day. Good day. I'm *going* to have a good day. Good day. Good day. Good day!"

Just then, Bruce the Australian exchange student walked by. His face lit up with a huge grin as Chang passed. "Well, g'day to you too, mate!" he said.

Chang headed toward the track behind the school. "I'll run a quick lap before the bell rings," he said. "That'll help me cool off." He set his backpack down and began to make the loop. But after only three steps, a huge chunk of flaming concrete fell from the sky and crushed him in the head, back, and neck.

"Oh my god!" exclaimed Mrs. Yectinbach, his first period Latin teacher. "What happened to you?"

"I'm fine," Chang mumbled through broken teeth and swollen lips. He dragged himself, hunched over, toward his seat, the singed filthy strips of wet pant legs trailing behind his bruised and bloody feet. "I'm actually having a really good day." He dropped his crushed backpack, still smoldering from the encounter with the flaming concrete, onto his desk and said, "I just need to go to the bathroom and freshen up."

Mrs. Yectinbach raised a suspicious eyebrow, but filled out a small yellow hall pass. "Okay," she said, "but hurry back. We're having a pop quiz today."

Chang froze. "A quiz?" he asked, his eyes filling with tears. He fell to his knees and shook angry fists at the heavens. "Nooooooooooooooo!"

The first sentence is the prompt. (Everyone writes the same basic story.) In my first draft Bob was homeless, but then I realized I was stigmatizing homelessness, and that's not cool. (I am now stigmatizing inbreeding, but whatever.) Every year the school where I teach changes the color of its hall passes, and I adjust my reading on the fly to match. Also I fell in love with the name "Mrs. Yectinbach" when I used it for the first time in this story. I continued to use it in later stories.

10. The Tapioca Canyon

The Grand Canyon was filled with tapioca pudding. I walked to the edge — not with the trepidation I'd had the day before, when there had been no pudding but only a terrifying precipice. I gazed down into the river of beige dessert food, then at my wife.

"Look, Sharon," I said. "The Grand Canyon is filled with tapioca pudding."

She gave me an annoyed look. "I can see that," she said. "Where did it come from?"

I shrugged. We heard the zipper of the tent open, and our son Malcolm emerged, yawning.

"Look, Malcolm," I said. "The Grand Canyon is filled with tapioca pudding."

He ran to join us. "Wow," he said. "Can I go swimming, mom?"

"I dunno," she said, and looked from the canyon to me. "Do you think it's safe?"

I shrugged. "All I know is, the Grand Canyon is filled with tapioca pudding."

Sharon sighed. "I guess it can't hurt," she said. As Malcolm ran to change into his swimsuit, a National Park Service truck pulled up.

A tall man in a brown uniform stepped out. "What's all this, then?" he asked.

I pointed into the goop. "The Grand Canyon is filled with tapioca pudding," I said.

Sharon scowled at me. "You just like saying that," she said.

I grinned. "Well, what *should* I say? You must admit, it's an amusing sentence. And after all, the Grand Canyon *is* filled with tapioca pudding."

"It's a sentence you certainly don't hear every day," she said.

"But imagine if you *did*," the park ranger said.

The next morning, the front page of the *New York Times* read: *Aliens invade Europe! Paris destroyed; millions dead!*

Another first-line prompt. I'm not sure why the park ranger is British; I think I had a student who loved Monty Python, so I threw it in. Maybe the ranger isn't actually British; maybe he just loves Monty Python too. When I finally had a student who asked what tapioca is, I realized I didn't actually know, so I had to look it up. (It comes from the cassava plant.)

11. Mah Teef

Cassandra sighed and picked up the phone. Ten minutes until quitting time. Tuesdays were so dumb — Mondays without the lingering fun of the weekend.

"Hello, thank you for calling Harkin, Smith, Kemblich, Yectinbach, Smith, and Johnson."

"AAA! My face!" The voice on the other end was a hideous screech of pain and noise. "My face! My back! My neck and my back!"

Cassandra sighed again. "Can I help you, *ma'am*?"

"Hey!" the person said. "I'm a *sir*. And I just got attacked by zombie werewolf vampires. I need help!"

Cassandra rolled her eyes. "Sir, this is a dental practice. I doubt we can help you."

He paused. "They broke all my teeth too!"

"Really. Because it sounds to me like your teeth are fine."

"Uh.. Uh.. No! Mah teef! Dere all bwoke! AAA! He'p me! I'm afwaid!"

"I'm sorry, sir, but I just do not believe you."

"I'm serious — uh, I mean.. I'm sewiuff! My teef awe all bwoken!" He began to sob.

"Yeah, well, it's a known fact that werewolves and vampires are forever locked in immortal conflict for control of the undead underworld. As for zombies, they take over whatever lifeform they infect. So a werewolf bitten by a zombie would stop *being* a werewolf. Same for vampires."

There was a pause. "Uh, okay. Well, can I make an appointment with the dentist?"

"You could have, two minutes ago, but now we're closed. Call back tomorrow and skip the fake zombie attack, okay?" She hung up, smiled, and headed out for the club.

The prompt: "A receptionist at a dentist's office answers the phone. The person on the other end is screaming in pain." Bonus points if you catch lines from <u>The Simpsons</u> and <u>Friday</u>.

12. In the Dumpster

"Hey! Hey! HEY HEY HEY! You're drippin' mustard on me, ya bacon-cheddar freak!" Baggy the bag of fries wiped the yellow goo from his side and scowled.

"Goodness," Patty the cheeseburger said. "I apologize profusely. Allow me to assist you." She moved toward him.

"Get away from me!" Baggy snapped. "You got all kinds of pickles and ketchup on you. I don't want none of that crap on me!"

Patty gave him a disapproving look. "I do wish you could choose less vulgar ways to express yourself," she said. "It's your crude appearance that got us into this debacle in the first place."

"Shove it," Baggy said. "Or I'll give you something to debacle about." He shook an angry fist.

Patty giggled. Baggy scowled. "What're you laughing about? Shut the bun up!"

"Well, it's quite clear that you're totally unfamiliar with the term 'debacle', as evidenced by your wholly incoherent use of the word."

"Oh yeah? How about the word 'shut up'?" Baggy growled. "Am I using that word right? As in shut your face in an upward direction?"

"No," Patty said.

"No what?"

"'Right' is an adjective, so it doesn't work there. You need to ask: 'Am I using that properly?' or use some other adverb."

"Ah, bite me," Baggy said.

"Don't mind if I do," said Fred the Homeless Guy, snatching up both Baggy and Patty and skipping merrily down the street.

Sometimes I'll just provide some characters and a setting and see what the students come up with. This one starts with a cheeseburger and a bag of fries in a dumpster. (Get it? Patty the cheeseburger?) I hoped that "Shut the bun up" would become the cool new thing to say around school, but so far it hasn't caught on.

13. The Evil Shoes

"I think my shoes are evil," she said, eyes darting wildly. Her hand was twitching around her iced mocha double latte whatever-the-crap she'd bought at Coffee Hut three minutes ago.

"You know what I think?" I said. "I think you're drinking too much coffee again."

"No way," she said, draining her cup. "This is only my third today."

I checked my watch. "Liz, it's seven-fifteen in the morning."

"I know," she said, pushing coins around in her hand. "I'm way behind." She frowned at the circles in her palm. "Can I borrow two bucks?"

I reached for my wallet, then froze. "Wait a minute," I said with narrowed eyes. "Is it for coffee?"

She looked around. "Uhh, no." I raised an eyebrow and waited. "Okay," she said finally. "Yes. I need another cup to get my brain moving."

"Forget it," I said, and sipped my tea.

She stood up suddenly, knocking her chair over onto the ground. "Was it the shoes?"

I scowled at her. "What?"

"Did my shoes tell you not to lend me money?" I rolled my eyes. "It was!" she yelled. "I knew it!" She put a shoe onto the metal table with a clang, ripped off the laces, then did the same with the other foot. She flung the shoes toward me and they landed two feet away. "Take 'em," she said. "I don't need you — I don't need *any* of you!" She ran toward Bob's Discount Coffee and disappeared inside.

Two minutes later she was traipsing slowly toward the table again, empty-handed and glum-faced. She was on the verge of tears.

"Would you like some tea?" I asked, holding out my custom-made Honoré de Balzac travel mug.

"No," she said. "That junk's barely got any caffeine at all." She sank back into her chair. "It's the shoes' fault," she mumbled.

Suddenly, she perked up, then rose in an instant and snatched her shoes from the floor. She ran toward Bob's Discount Coffee again.

I heard her yelling: "Bob! Hey Bob! You wanna buy a pair of shoes? They're not evil or nothin' — I promise!"

I drink two cups of coffee each morning, so I know I'm addicted. But it's scary how much caffeine some people suck down every day. The title is a nod to Steve Martin's book <u>The Cruel Shoes</u>. Also: The shoes landed two feet away, get it?

14. The Weekly Arm

"Did you read his arm yesterday?" Kelly asked.

I sat up in my desk. "No. What was the headline?" Gustav's arm-based newspaper, *The Weekly Arm*, was my main source of news. I never missed an issue.

Kelly gave that little smug smirk of hers. "You'll just have to read it yourself."

"Oh come *on*," I said. "Just tell me."

"Why don't you get a subscription?" she asked. For twenty dollars a month, Gustav would find you on the day of publication and roll up his sleeve.

"I can't afford that," I said. "C'mon, Kelly. Just tell me."

She smirked and shook her head. Her plastic earrings flopped around. "Sorry, Fred, no dice. But it's a really good story."

I grimaced. "Augh," I said. "Now I've got to know."

She giggled. "Ha ha, I know and you don't."

I thought for a moment, tapping my pencil. An idea struck and I raised my hand. "Mrs. Yectinbach," I said, "can I go to the bathroom?"

Mrs. Yectinbach peered at me. "Have you finished your translation, Fred?"

I looked at my paper. "This is ridiculous. How do you expect us to translate all 2200 pages of Proust's *À la recherche du temps perdu* in one class period?" I threw down my pencil. "I don't even speak French!"

"Yeah," Kelly added. "Why are we doing this in gym class, anyway?"

"Do two more pages and you can go," Mrs. Y said.

I grumbled and tried another sentence. It was no use — the whole page was just jumbled letters.

Kelly leaned over. "You're gonna die when you read his arm," she said. "It is *such* a cool story!"

"Stop!" I said. "You're gonna make me crazy."

"It's out of this world," she said. "Your jaw will literally drop."

"Augh!" I cried, jumping up and running from the room. Mrs. Y gave chase, both of us stampeding through the hallway. I dashed toward the math rooms. *Third hour*, I thought. *He's in geometry class*. With Mrs. Y in hot pursuit — followed by two security officers and an assistant principal — I blasted through the doors of Room 220. I spotted Gustav near the window, putting the final touches on a chocolate cake. I leaped and tackled him to the ground, sending chocolate icing and egg whites flying.

"What is the meaning of this?" Mr. Kemlioff shouted. The guards and Mrs. Yectinbach raced in, but I ignored them and pinned Gustav to the floor. "I've got to know!" I shouted. "Let me read your arm!"

"You didn't pay!" Gustav cried. "Let go of me!"

"No!" I yelled. "Lemme see!" I managed to grab his sleeve and yanked it up. I seized his arm and held it still long enough to read the headline: *Kelly drives Fred crazy with misleading info about this week's news! 15-year-old student faces suspension for insubordination, attacking another student, and disrupting geometry class.*

I started to cry.

I actually heard a student say the first line one day in the hall. Room 220 was my first high-school classroom.

15. Never Be Forgot

"3.. 2.. 1.. HAPPY NEW YEAR!" Bobby cheered with excitement, spinning his noisemaker wildly as he jumped around the room, blowing through his horn with "2013" in bright red letters on the side. Emily smiled but plugged her ears against the racket.

Bobby hit *Play* on his mp3 player and the familiar strains of "Auld Lang Syne" filled the room. He grabbed the bottle of champagne and held it toward Emily. "D'you want to do the honors?" he asked.

"No thanks," she said. "Would you turn that down?" She gestured to the mp3 device.

"What?" he shouted, and popped the cork. "Turn it up? Sure!" He slid the volume level to maximum and filled two glasses. He held one toward Emily but she gave him a sour look.

"You're kidding, right?" she asked

"Suit yourself," he said, and looked around the room. Alas, no one else had the New Year's Spirit, either. Everyone looked completely bored. *Worst party ever*, he thought. He downed the glass of champagne and gave the noisemaker a few more rambunctious spins.

Suddenly the CEO, Mr. Abberjacky, came barreling out of his office into the cubicle workroom. "What in tarnation is going on out here?" he yelled. "Jenkins, you're fired. I know you suffer from chronic temporal amnesia, but I can't have you disrupting work all the time just because you think it's New Year's Eve! It's the middle of June, for crying out loud." He yanked the cable out of the mp3 player, handed it to Bobby, and pointed to the door.

"Wow," Emily said. "That was a much more coherent firing speech than I would have given." She watched as Bobby, still spinning his noisemaker — only now with great languor and woe — trudged out of the office forever.

My first student teacher put the first line of dialogue on the board one day for Journal Writing. I couldn't find a way to reveal the punchline without info-dumping, so I just dumped and then let Emily make a joke out of it.

16. The Secret

He leaned over to me. "Can you keep a secret?" he asked.

I paused, then said: "This better be important." The previews had just ended; we were about to start our fifth viewing of *The Matrix Reloaded*.

"It is," he whispered. "Cornel West is in this movie."

"*I know!*" I shouted as the movie theatre's logo danced on the screen. "We've seen this movie together four times already, and every time you tell me that Cornel West is in the freakin' movie! I know Cornel West is in the movie! You point him out to me when he's on the screen and you say 'Look — it's Cornel West!' Shut the hell up about Cornel West already! Yeah, he's a cool guy, but I'm starting to hate him because *you* won't clam up about him. Every time someone asks us what we think of this movie, you start yammering on about Cornel West. Cornel West. Give it a rest, would you? And you'd *better* not recite his lines while he's saying them, like you did last time. Everyone around us was shushing us because you were talking during the movie! Then you got down in the aisle and started saying 'Hail Counselor West' and bowing toward the screen. It's pathetic! Shut up already, would you? Just *shut up!*"

I sat back down and scowled as the opening credits began. Several moviegoers looked at me with odd expressions, but I didn't care.

Then the girl next to us leaned over and whispered: "Dude! Did you say Cornel West is in this movie?"

He smiled at me, then nodded vigorously to her and gave her a thumbs-up. She grinned and said "Sweet! I love that guy."

This is based on a true story. (The first line is the prompt.) I had no idea Cornel West was in the second <u>Matrix</u> movie, so I got very very excited when he appeared on the screen, embarrassing my wife to death. Then a guy in the next row leaned over and said "Is that Cornel West?" and I nodded with joy.

17. The Giant Talking Lizard Bird

The pterodactyl gestured with its head. It wanted me to climb on its back. "I can't believe this!" I cried. It gestured again, as if to nod. It almost seemed like it was smiling. Where had it come from? Why had it chosen me?

I didn't know — all I knew was that I was about to have the most fantastic experience of my life.

As I sat across its enormous wings, the creature soared into the air. The ground fell away and I held on with a giddy rush as euphoria swept through me. Then, even more amazing, the giant lizard bird talked.

"So," it said in a raspy voice, "where shall we go?"

Stunned, thrilled, and breathless, and said: "I dunno. This is all so tremendous!"

"There's a performance of the opera *Bizet*," it said. "We could go see that."

"Uhh," I said.

"Or we could go down to the library and see what new books they've gotten in recently."

"Yeah, that's really dumb," I said. "Why don't we go fight some other dinosaurs?"

"What other dinosaurs?"

"I don't know. Aren't there some other dinosaurs around somewhere?"

"Just my mom—"

"Well, let's go fight—"

"I am *not* going to fight my mom."

"Fine. How about the Blue Angels?" I said. "They're performing over the state capitol today. I bet you could take down two or three of those suckers."

It twisted its head to shoot me a confused, angry glare. "You want me to attack a steel jet plane?"

I threw up my hands and nearly fell off. "Well *I* don't know! Let's do *something*."

One hour later, we were parked in the uncomfortable wooden chairs of a lecture hall, listening to a 90-year-old bald guy talk about the textiles of ancient Mesopotamia.

"This sucks," I said.

"Shhh," the pterodactyl hissed at me. "I'm trying to hear this."

It was the most boring day of my life.

The prompt: "Write a story about a child who meets a talking dinosaur." In case you can't tell, I like to drive these stories in the opposite direction from the standard expectation. I'm endlessly amused by action stories that are dull and boring.

18. Flappin'

There's this guy, and he's flappin' his arms, and he goes: "Yes! terday I was flappin' my dog's arms!"

"What are you talking about?" asked the judge. The entire courtroom was peering at the guy with inflamed curiosity.

"You know," he said, "my dog's arms. He goes dancin' the la bambaaa.." As he began to sing, the guy rose to his feet and sashayed around the courtroom. His lawyer sank her head into her hands.

The judge banged his gavel. "Mister President," he said. "This is highly unorthodox."

But the president couldn't hear the judge. He was lost in his own tiny little world, a world of wood sprites and gumdrop munchkins, where ducks shoot grapes at hammers and all the world's a big bathtub filled with tofu-based snack treats.

"Bailiff," the judge said, "please escort the witness back to the stand." But it was too late. The president was dancing right out the doors of the courtroom and disappeared into the hallway. The judge was about to declare a mistrial, when the doors suddenly slammed open once again, and there stood the president — with Marie Antoinette beside him!

All the spectators gasped in astonishment, then exploded with spontaneous applause. It was a great day for America. Marie Antoinette was a caveman.

This one is in the "Don't ask me" category. I just turned on the weird faucet and let it happen. The first line comes from an inside joke a friend tells about someone who couldn't tell a joke properly. I really enjoy reading this one to the class.

19. The Killer Mutant Survival Guide

"Dude, why bother? Books are so *boring*," Tom said.

Agent Stern blinked, still holding out *The Killer Mutant Survival Guide*. "Sir," he said, "trust me. You're going to want to read this." He thrust it toward Tom again.

Tom took it and frowned at the plain beige cover. "This looks stupid," he said, and flipped through it. "Where are the pictures? I like books with pictures."

Agent Stern sighed. "Sir," he said, "I really don't have time for this. There is a horde of deadly vicious killer mutants on their way into the city." He pointed to the survival guide and shifted the weight of the huge sack on his shoulder. "This book will give you essential information to help you avoid them and stay alive. If you don't want to have your eyeballs chewed out and get strangled with your own intestines by radioactive demon creatures, then *read this book*."

Tom let out a pained groan. "Damn," he cried. "Three hundred pages?" He shook his head. "Isn't there an audio book? Did they make a movie about—"

"*No!*" Agent Stern shouted. "There's no movie. There's no audiobook. Read this book if you want to live through the end of the week. Now if you'll excuse me, I've got five hundred more books to distribute today." He stormed off to the next house.

Tom made a face and tossed the book toward the garbage can. "What*ever*," he said. "I'm not readin' no stupid three-hundred-page book." He flipped the channel past the news.

"Rampaging monsters have been sighted on the outskirts of—"

"Boring!" Tom said, and turned to the football game.

I really do think it would come to this for some people. Once a student loudly declared to me that he would never read a book in his life. I know I was lucky to grow up in such an intellectually nurturing home, but the level of aliteracy I see in many young people can be shocking. The prompt is the first line of dialogue.

20. The Freezer

Mary thought her kid was possessed and put her baby in the freezer. Little Jacob was *not*, in fact, possessed — at least not by the devil, or any other evil force — but he was cold. So cold, in fact, that he began to worry about frostbite and hypothermia.

Fortunately, Jacob was a very resourceful child. He immediately crawled over to the temperature dial and spun it all the way to the warmest possible setting. This wasn't very warm — it was a freezer, after all — but soon it felt a little better. Then Jacob arranged several boxes of fish sticks into a rudimentary igloo and huddled inside it for warmth. This helped a little more, and he was proud of his ingenuity.

Jacob was still cold, so he ventured out of his fishstick igloo for other ways to make himself more comfortable. He found a bag of tater-tots and tucked it under one arm, and grabbed a box of Cracker Jacks with his free hand. He took these to the igloo and opened them up. He crawled inside the tater-tot pouch and found that it made quite a decent sleeping bag. Soon his toes were toasty warm. But the rest of him was shivering and cold. So he opened the Cracker Jacks and prayed that the free prize inside would be something useful for staying warm.

Much to his delight he discovered, at the bottom of the box, a "Lil' Scout Junior Campfire Kit". It came with kindling, two firewood logs, and a lighter.

He broke an icicle off the roof of the freezer and used it to poke a hole in the top of his igloo, then kept going until there was a hole in the top of the freezer itself, so the smoke could escape. Then he set up his campfire in the middle of the igloo and snuggled into his tater-tot sleeping bag. As the bite-sized potato chunks slowly roasted around him, the aroma of starchy goodness wafted around the igloo and Jacob drifted off into a lovely warm sleep.

Then later his father Tyrone pulled him out of the freezer and Mary started seeing a therapist and Jacob grew up to be the mayor of Murfreesboro, Tennessee.

The first line was submitted to me on a form I made called "Journal Writing Topic Suggestion". I'm always worried that some kids might make horribly violent stories and I'll have to bring them in for a chat with the guidance counselor, but that's possible no matter what the prompt is. Still, I decided to make my story a happy ending. I try to avoid using actual brand names, but in this case I don't think anyone would understand what a box of "Poppy Jacks" was, much less why it had a prize inside.

21. Three Days

Angelo smiled as the bell rang. He was stoked for the three-day weekend. It was so much free time, all splayed out before him. He was going to play so much *Warfield 2: Battle Combat*. True, he had work to do — plenty, in fact. He had quizzes to grade and essays to read, and he'd agreed to write an article for a local newsweekly as well. But all that could wait. For now, he was free.

Of course, he'd probably end up — as always, when the end of the year came — scrambling at the last minute to get everything done. But all he could taste now was the sweet nectar of release. He would go — he could just run. The world was spread out like a new bookstore that had just opened.

He paused, took a deep breath, and closed his eyes as the sun warmed his face. Walking out of the building, he felt like Ruben "Hurricane" Carter (played by Denzel Washington), looking up at the everloving sun as it beat down on him on his first day out of prison. It was an unshackling, the feel of this Friday afternoon, and he murmured a prayer of thanks for the beatific weather.

He stumbled to his car in a half-daze, worried that he should drink in every instant of euphoria in which he swam. We never appreciate fun while it's going on, he knew. And when it's over, we can only look back and wish we were there again. But the moment *before*.. The glorious precipice of anticipation — therein lay the most thorough ecstasy of our lives.

I usually take silly or absurd approaches to the prompts. But I wrote this on the last day before a three-day weekend, and I like the way it captures the emotional texture of the situation. The first sentence is the prompt.

22. Noonan Beach

The sun was creeping over the horizon, a lazy stalker shambling toward a blurry target. Simon sighed and shifted the weight of his hand around the grip of the briefcase. *It's like me*, he thought. *Ra and Sol — endless cycles, fatigue and duty*. He glanced around to make sure he was still alone.

"Noonan Beach," the old voice on the recording had said. "Sunrise." *Well, here I am. It's sunrise. I did everything I was supposed to do. Now show up, please, and take this damn thing off of me.*

It had only been four months, but it felt like two years. Running, walking, driving, hiding. Being ordered around by faceless commandments, mangled by digital noise and distortion. *I need time to rest*, he thought, and then immediately: *A long time to rest. I've had short rests, but those felt like tiny breathers*. Even when the heat was off, he knew it would snap back again, and he'd be right back into the fire.

It wasn't all bad. When it was over, he knew, he would remember it well. Probably hang onto nothing but the positives. There had been plenty of good times and good things, and he was grateful for them. He knew, too, that the whole thing served a good purpose. He had chosen to be here; chosen to have this cursed black box chained to his arm; chosen to stand here in the hazy light of dawn with a metal curve digging into his wrist.

But right now he was sick of it. He was sick of the confusing instructions. Sick of the people he had to meet with, refusing to cooperate, demanding to know what was in it for them. Like the guy in the blue SUV. "I know I signed up for it," he'd told Simon. "But I gotta get my money."

"This box will get you money," Simon had said, holding it out. But the guy wouldn't take it. Simon had wanted to smack him. Instead he gnashed his teeth and waited. The guy made a call, then told Simon to rearrange the stuff in the box. More horsecrap. But he had to get the guy to take the box, so he started rearranging. Then the guy made him do it again. Finally, repeating this nonsense four times, the guy took the box and peeled out. Never said thanks, never apologized for wasting Simon's time.

Every day it was something similar. Making him wait, making him do extra work. Simon wondered where they found these people. Sometimes it seemed like they were chosen solely on the basis of how much difficulty and frustration they were likely to cause for Simon.

He shook his head and blinked twice. He glanced at his wrist before he remembered about losing his watch. He sat down on the sand and dropped the case beside him and let his right arm rest a little. Couldn't move it much, but at least the pressure was off. But it hurt. Some kind of stinging in the middle. Probably something about the carpal tunnel.

"Hey!" a raspy voice cried out to his left. He peered at the rocks near the parking lot and saw a short man wearing an orange windbreaker. "Are you Simon?" he shouted.

"Y—" Simon was more exhausted than he realized. He had to clear his throat before he could speak. "Yeah," he called out. The man hopped over a rock and shambled toward him, clutching a white garbage bag. Simon rose to his feet and sighed. "Please tell me you've got a key in there," he said.

"Nope," the man said with a sloppy grin. He dug into his left pocket and pulled out a crumpled, dirty scrap of paper. "But they said we'll get a key when we bring them all the stuff on this list." He thrust it toward Simon, who closed his eyes a little and let out a weak breath.

Two purple napkins. A dead turtle. Fifty-two North Dakota shot glasses. Simon looked at the man and shook his head a little. "It's never going to stop," he said quietly. The man just peered at him, eyes scrunched up. "This will never, ever stop, will it?"

The man shrugged and displayed his sloppy grin again. "I guess not," he said.

The prompt here is: "A man in a business suit, briefcase handcuffed to his wrist, stands on a quiet beach, watching the sun rise." This is often how I feel at the end of the school year. I love my job and I cannot imagine doing anything else for a living. But the intransigence, the obstinacy, the endless jumping through hoops of all kinds — these things wear on me until I feel like Simon here.

23. Style Kit

"Hey, yo — I want my money back!" Billy said. "You said this thing would get me a recording contract."

Steve the Clerk looked down at the InstaRapper™ Gangsta Style Kit. "Sir, we said it could *help* get you a contract, if used properly." He pointed to a red circle on the front of the box. "See, right here it says 'Fresh rhymes not included'. You have to provide your own."

"Yo, F that," Billy growled. "I memorized all the slang sayings in the phrasebook there, I got my pants hangin' crazy low" — he gestured to his floppy jeans, nestled around his kneecaps, showing off his Spider-Man boxer shorts — "and I've been throwing money around all day. See?" He took out a sweaty roll of one-dollar bills from his pocket, peeled off four of them, and tossed them playfully at Steve. "I'm makin' it rain, baby!" Billy yelled.

Steve sighed. "Sir, I'm sorry, but hip-hop is not something you can get out of a box. It's a culture, like punk or country or breakbeat or opera. It's more than just the music and how you dress. Like Brother Ali said: 'gotta earn respect to brag and boast / skills get you that, not swag and clothes'."

"Yo, F that," Billy said.

Steve blinked. "What?" he asked, waiting for Billy to continue. Instead he just shrugged.

"I dunno," he said. "The phrasebook said I'm supposed to say 'F that' if I don't agree or don't understand something."

"Well you know what? You and you and your background dancer are going to have to leave," Steve said.

Billy sighed again. "C'mon, Susie," he said to the bikini babe gyrating her pelvis nearby. He looked at Steve once more with sad eyes. "F that," he said again, and walked out.

I think the first line was another student suggestion. As a middle-aged white guy, I feel strange lecturing teenagers about what hip-hop really is. But many of them simply do not get it.

24. Narrative Stream Sense

"Fish the door flap track," she said. "Car sign-21. Bubblegum tractor pig."

"Yeah," I said, exasperated. "But Green Bay yahoo concrete sulphur stick gone bag buffalo."

She shook her head. "No good," she said, and sang the bucket green style ship. "Look," she continued. "My this you buddy exhaust purple sky." When after next cosmic splatter frog hopping clouds.

For neverskip? Almost — 44 to eternity. Rocks in eyeball nose lobe quality. "Quality!" I shouted, and swam about liver circles drop the hi-lo Treelo in a quart shoebox beatbox. "Sweat socks," I said.

She eyes tears welled. "For three to have won," she whispered. "Narrative stream sense since before forever."

"Hold it," I said. "You're starting to make a little sense."

She rolled her eyes. "Dingbat frosted auxiliary," she said. "Graphite finger foods smirkingly." The bus walked by. She rose and raised a thorn. "Gleeb-fram! Bagooma feeber foober!"

"Well, if you're going to be *silly*," I said.

She gasped and looked up. "No," she said with a flourish. "Never to my love." She ran up and hugged me."

"Who did?" I asked.

But her eyes were far away. She didn't answer.

"Who?" I repeated.

She looked at me, a thin, watery gaze. Her heart was in her face and I nearly collapsed with the pain of her eyes. Her soul was dry.

I wrote the first line of dialogue as a prompt during my first year of teaching and created this story in response. I can't figure out why, but I really like it. Partly of course it's the sheer absurdity of it, but there's something real and heartfelt here, too. I'm not good at writing actual poetry, but I like how this turned out as a blend of poetic license and prose.

25. Algebron

"Dude, there is no such thing as Algebron," Bob said, flipping his pen around in his hand. "You can't just make up alien planets."

Lucius rose to his feet and pointed an accusing finger at Bob. "SPEAK NOT TO ME OF FICTIONAL PLANETOIDS!" he thundered. "THINE EYES SEE NOT THE HORRORS BEYOND THIS TERRESTRIAL PRISON!"

"Would you pipe *down*?" Bob said, trying to hide behind his science textbook. "We're in a freaking library, man. And sit down before you fall down."

"I STAND FOR THE GLORY OF ALL MATHEMATICAL SYSTEMS THROUGHOUT OUR MANY UNIVERSES!" Lucius raised his arms aloft, tilting his head upward.

"That doesn't make any sense," Bob said. "'Uni' means 'one', so how can there be many universes?"

"YOUR FEEBLE HUMAN MIND CANNOT COMPREHEND THE MULTIDIMENSIONAL TRUTHS OF THIS GALACTIC NIGHTMARE IN WHICH YOUR

PUNY PLANET DRIFTS, AIMLESS AND DOOMED BY THE COSMIC SHIFTS OF THE SPACETIME CONTINUUM!" He began to cackle with glee, his belly jiggling beneath his blue and purple robe.

"Okay," Bob said. "Whatever. Now shut up so I can get ready for this quiz I have to take next hour." He jotted down some words in his spiralbound notebook. Lucius sat down and glanced over at Bob's notes, then suddenly rose again and pointed at the book.

"THE HUMAN FIELD OF BIOLOGY IS A FRAUD AND A DISGRACE," Lucius yelled. "THE ILLUSORY FARCE YOU CALL 'THE ANIMAL KINGDOM' IS FAR MORE COMPLEX THAN YOUR PATHETIC MINDS COULD EVER COMPREHEND! ABANDON YOUR RIDICULOUS, CLUMSY, AND ERRONEOUS EFFORTS TO UNDERSTAND THIS UNIVERSE!"

"Dude, *shut up*," Bob hissed. "Mrs. Yectinbach is coming over here."

"VERY WELL," Lucius said, glancing over his shoulder. "I SHALL LEAVE YOU TO THIS JUVENILE IDIOCY. SIMPLY LOAN ME ONE OF YOUR EARTH DOLLARS SO I MAY PURCHASE A CANDY BAR FILLED WITH SUGAR, CARBOHYDRATES, AND EMPTY CALORIES. THEN I WILL PROVIDE THE SILENCE YOUR PUNY MINDS SO DESPERATELY SEEK!"

Bob pulled a crumpled bill out of his pocket and flung it on the table. "Here," he said. "Now get out of here."

"I ASSUME YOU WILL BE PRESENT IN THE POST-MERIDIEM SEGMENT OF THIS EARTH DAY, AT THE RITUALISTIC EXERCISE FOR CLUB AND SPHERE ENHANCEMENT?"

Bob rolled his eyes. "Yeah, I'll be at baseball practice." He waved a hand. "Now get lost."

"THEN I SHALL SEE YOU THERE!" Lucius bellowed, and threw a tiny device at the ground. A cloud of smoke appeared, and he ran for the exit.

"We can all still see you," a girl at the next table yelled. "Ya loud weirdo!" Bob held up his hand and she slapped him a hi-five.

The first line was another suggestion from a student. The sporty kids get a kick out of the phrase "club and sphere enhancement". I love reading Lucius' dialogue at full volume, much to the chagrin of whichever teacher is unlucky enough to be trapped next door.

26. Tyconderson Industries

"Get over here, you thief!" the young woman shouted, blasting Simon J. Tyconderson with her patented Anti-Crime Quik-Freez™ gel. He was frozen in place, one hand on his cell phone and the other clutching a bag of money with a dollar sign on it.

"My word!" Tyconderson said in his ridiculously posh accent. "How *dare* you call me a thief. I am merely a businessman, seeking to maximize profit in the free market." He gestured — as best he could — to his stock portfolio on the desk nearby.

"Free market!?" the woman trilled. "You mean government *subsidy*! You got a hundred and twenty million dollars from the Department of Agriculture last year, and your company relies desperately on state and local law enforcement to make your profits. Tyconderson Industries would go bankrupt tomorrow in a *real* free market."

"Bah!" Tyconderson said with a sneer. "You simply wish to punish success, you silly girl. You're just jealous that I worked so hard to achieve my vast fortune."

"You pay your workers eight bucks an hour while giving yourself a two million dollar bonus for foreclosing on old ladies' houses, even though the workers do all the actual work! You may have worked hard in the past, but who's making the wealth for Tyconderson Industries now?"

He giggled. "Why, sixteen-year-olds in my Chinese sweatshops, of course! But if we weren't offering jobs, they would have *no* opportunities."

"Yeah, and if the Chinese government didn't bust independent unions, they'd have a shot at a living wage." She chucked him into a nearby paddy wagon and said "Get him outta my sight!"

I try to leave politics out of my fiction Journal Writing, but when a student submitted the first line here as a prompt, I couldn't resist. I have no idea how Tyconderson Industries actually makes money, but that's a bad company. He's probably friends with Montgomery Burns.

27. The Turkey Hat

I fidgeted. It was late. I'd been in Big Fred's Super Hat Warehouse for over two hours, and I was starting to get cranky. I was in the Cap — Humorous/Mechanical wing, but every hat I saw had some problem with it. This one with the clapping hands was such a cliché. That beer helmet was very Homer Simpson, but it was a boring (and ugly) orange. And the less said about the tractor cap, the better.

To make matters worse, some woman with three wailing kids kept trying on hat after hat after hat, paying no more mind to her squealing rugrats than one might to a dog sniffing in the grass while out for a walk. They were shattering my concentration, but she didn't seem to care. I wasn't going to leave — I was there first! She should take her screaming snotbags and go back to the kids' hats at the north end of the store.

Then I saw it — The Holy Grail of wacky hats. It was grey, with a big turkey torso sticking out the front, and pair of floppy (but sturdy) wings on the side. A simple pullstring sat at chin-level. I put it on and moved in front of the mirror. The lady, recognizing my truly wondrous find, moved aside with an awed expression. I flapped the wings and nearly cried. This was *it*.

The next day at school, I was the darling of show and tell. As I withdrew the hat from my book bag, the class erupted into "ooh"s and "ahh"s. When I flapped the wings, the entire room applauded, teacher included.

From that day forward, I *ran* the playground. No longer did the bully Joey ask me for my milk money — indeed, he started offering cash to *me* in exchange for the right to stand near me and my glorious hat during recess.

This is based on a true hat. I had that hat during middle school, and while it did not imbue me with lovely social magic as in the story, it was a really cool hat. The prompt for this one is: "Write a story about someone shopping for a hat."

28. Happy Time

"Try new Spider Larvae Cereal!" I said, my enormous grin giving lie to the seven hours I'd spent on the street today without a single sale. The lady slammed the door shut, missing my nose by less than an inch.

Make big money, the ad had promised. Door-to-door cereal sales was the best way to achieve financial independence, I had been told. It wasn't until I'd gotten my first case of product — and paid five hundred dollars to invest — that I realized what I would be selling.

Customers (to put it nicely) just weren't interested. One old guy actually threw up on my shoes when I showed him the box. One kid seemed interested, but when he asked his mother for the three bucks, she threatened to call the police and report me as a pederast.

Along with the first case of "cereal", the Happy Time Food Company had sent a brochure entitled *Winning Ways: Ten Tips for Success in Sales*, promising to give me the skills I would need to move the merchandise. Confidence, appearance, and persistence were the keys, it said. So I gave it a shot.

Now, three weeks later, I'd only sold six boxes. The other 494 were becoming moldy in the kitchen area of my tiny one-room apartment. Worse, some of the larvae were becoming adult spiders, crawling around in my bed and underpants drawer.

Depressed, I sat awake at 3:00 AM, flipping through the channels. Crap. Crap. Garbage. Crap. Hello, what's this? Achieve economic security today. Easy product sales guarantee you big money now. These eyeball injection kits are sure to sell like hotcakes. Call the Happy Time Food Company today!

I ran to the phone, credit card in hand.

I want to know who bought the six boxes and why. I think I came up with the first line as a prompt, just trying to be weird. Mission accomplished!

29. Ms. McKratzenvimmer

Gloria spat. "Oh yeah?" she shouted. "Well, so's your grandma!" She gave the cop a shove. No one was going to get away with calling *her* an octogenarian — badge or no badge.

The cop took a step back and withdrew his club. "Ma'am," he said, "calm down. You're hysterical."

Gloria spat. "Oh yeah?" she shouted. "Well, so's your grandma!"

Three days later, she stood beside her court-appointed lawyer. The judge looked at her file, then at her. "Gloria McKratzenvimmer," he said, "you've been charged with assault of a police officer and willful endangerment. However, it's clear that you're too mentally disturbed to stand trial."

Gloria spat. "Oh yeah?" she shouted. "Well, so's your grandma!"

After the judge found her in contempt of court, her lawyer turned to face her. "You must be crazy to talk to a judge like that."

Gloria spat. "Oh yeah?" she shouted. "Well, so's your grandma!"

Five years later, Gloria was the first woman to walk on the moon. As the world watched in hushed awe, the words of radio transmission shot around the globe.

"Ms. McKratzenvimmer," the ground control engineer said, "you've achieved a great victory for all humankind. You are a shining light to all the people of Earth."

Gloria spat inside her helmet. ""Oh yeah?" she shouted, her words scratchy through the void of space. "Well, so's your grandma!"

I think the first line was a prompt suggestion from a student. I'd just like to say that "McKratzenvimmer" is the second best surname I've ever come up with.

30. The Maniac from Vegetable Hill

"Omigod!" Lonnie froze just inside the front door and gripped his sister's arm. "Katherine! Who's that freakazoid in dad's chair?" He gestured around the corner, where a balding, overweight guy in baggy jeans and a greasy blue shirt sat slumped in their father's overstuffed recliner.

Katherine was shaking. "I dunno, I dunno, I dunno." She rocked back and forth.

"What should we do?" Lonnie whispered, a tense little hiss.

Katherine continued to rock. "I dunno, I dunno, I dunno." Her lips were trembling.

Suddenly the man leaped up and shouted. "Ah HA!" he cried. "*There* you are!" He raced to the door and stood in front of it. The children squealed and darted for the back hallway. "There's nowhere to run!" he called after them, lumbering toward their bedroom. He flung the door wide and spewed a sick, guttural laugh into the room. It sank down below the bunk beds, where Lonnie and Katherine were hiding, their tiny hands grasping each other for dear life.

The man in the greasy blue shirt stopped in the middle of the room. "I know you're in here," he said to the air. "You can't run from me."

Katherine began to whimper, her wet sobs lost between a painful thick moan of horror. The man dropped to his knees and gazed under the bed. "Ah HA!" he barked, and pointed a finger into the darkness where they were cowering. The kids began to scream, but stifled themselves with panic. "I understand two very naughty children haven't been eating their vegetables!"

More screaming, and then Lonnie stopped. "Wait. What?"

The man in the greasy blue shirt said "Yes! I'm the maniac from Vegetable Hill!" He flexed his fingers with a twisted glee. "I'm the one who will find you, and tear your face off, unless you eat your vegetables for dinner!"

Katherine began moaning and crying again, then she called out: "Mommy! Help!"

Lonnie's eyes were wide with curious fury. "You sick weirdo!" he yelled from the darkness under the bed. "Leave us alone!" He looked toward the bedroom door as the familiar shadows of their mother and father came into the room.

"Okay, Carl," their mother said. "That'll be enough for today." The man in the greasy blue shirt stood up. Their parents knelt down and smiled at Lonnie and Katherine. "You can come out now," she said soothingly.

Lonnie froze and grabbed Katherine to keep her from leaving the safety zone. "What in *the world* is going on?"

"Carl here is a friend of mine," their father said. "He's an actor with the local theater group. We asked him to come by and scare you kids a little."

The man in the greasy blue shirt waved at the kids, now peering out from the edge of the bed, and took a small bow.

"We want you to be healthy," their mother said. "We thought this might be a good way to scare you straight."

Their dad smiled. "Whenever you think maybe you don't want to finish your green beans, remember how scared you were when Carl started running after you."

Katherine shook loose from her brother's grip and slithered toward her mother. "Mommy," she said. "I peed my pants."

"I know," her mother said, giving her a hug while trying not to let her get too close.

"We figured you'd be pretty scared," their dad said, "but it seemed like the only way."

Katherine looked over at Lonnie. "Got it?" Her brother was pushing buttons on his cell phone.

"Got it," he said, and played the last few seconds back to be sure. His father's voice came from the tiny device: "... it seemed like the only way."

Their dad looked at their mom. "What the?"

The bedroom door banged open once again and a woman in a business suit, carrying a briefcase, marched into the room. "Deborah Jenkins," she announced. "Child Protective Services." She thrust a sheet of paper into their father's hand. "This is a summons. Your son here just called me to report your horrible parenting." She looked him up and down. "You ought to be ashamed of yourself, scaring little kids like this."

Their mother jumped up. "The basement," she said quickly. "Go lock the basement before she looks down there!"

But Deborah Jenkins just laughed, and soon the kids were laughing too. "Relax," she said. "I'm not really from Child Protective Services. I'm an actor with Carl at the theater group." She and Carl slapped hi-fives. "When I found out about what you and he were planning, I arranged with the kids to set up something for you, too."

"Well," their mother said, finally relaxing into a smile. "I guess we all learned a lesson today about what we're doing wrong in life."

"We sure did," Lonnie and Katherine said in unison.

After paying the actors, the family went out to Chuck-E-Cheese to celebrate and laugh about their crazy night.

The prompt: "Two children come home to find a strange man asleep in their father's easy chair." When I read this one to the class, I end with a happy voice and try to move quickly into the day's lesson. I keep a straight face until someone asks "What's in the basement!?" but you'd be surprised how often no one asks — I guess because they weren't listening, or they're too shy to speak up, or they think they missed something.

31. This Sucks

Tony shoved Mike aside and said "I'm fine."

Mike sighed. "No, you're not," he said. "Give 'em up." He held out his hand, but Tony just grinned, like an idiot. A stupid, gap-toothed cretin. He lunged past Mike and fumbled into the lock.

From behind them, someone shouted. "Hey!" It was Jen. "What's going on?"

Tony closed his eyes and let out a long, angry breath. He looked toward her, then quickly away. He threw the keys on the ground and stormed back toward the house. "Fine," he said. "Whatever."

Susan balled up her napkin with the hamburger wrapper. "I don't effin' care," she said, drawing her soda. "We're her freakin' friends. You do *not* do that to your friends."

Karen fidgeted. "But if she'd told everyone, it wouldn't have worked—"

"No," Susan snapped. She jabbed a finger toward Karen. "She made it very clear who her real friends are, and we didn't make the list." She sat back. "You wanna hang out with her, go ahead. As far as I'm concerned, it actually happened." She crossed her arms and drew soda. "I'm done."

Dave dropped the phone. It clattered on the hardwood floor. After a few seconds, Mike's voice came through. "Dave?" he said. "You there?"

This Ain't What You Rung For

Dave was staring at the fireplace. He was in the family room. He looked down at his red bracelet, then at the phone. "Dave," Mike said in a tinny, faraway squawk. "Dave, what happened?"

Zombie-style, Dave picked it up. "I'm here," he said. His voice was thin and insubstantial; watery.

"Yeah, I know, right?" Mike said. "They only told a few people."

"Who?"

"Angela, Mary, Rachel, Ronnie. Steve."

Dave blinked; he couldn't think of anything else to do. "So they were all acting?"

"Yep."

"And her parents? Mr. Keyser?" He scowled. "The freakin' *cops*?"

"Yeah, all the way down."

"I cannot freakin' *believe* this," Dave said.

Mike sighed. "Believe it," he said.

Mike leaned back in his chair. "This sucks," he announced to no one in particular. "Why do we have to have homeroom today?" Susan smiled and worked through another geometry problem. "Yeah, really," she said.

Ms. Lopez let out a slow breath. "I need your attention, everyone." She waited a second. "Susan, please put the math down for a minute."

Susan rolled her eyes and shut the book. Hesitantly, she looked at Ms. Lopez.

"Now, today's homeroom is for everyone in the school, but I know you two were friends with Jen."

Susan looked at Mike quickly, then away just as quickly. The last two weeks had been a blur. She fingered her red wristband. "Yeah," she said quietly. "What about her?"

The Fiction Journal

From out in the hall, a shriek slammed into the door. Susan looked up at Mike, but he was just as confused as she.

Ms. Kinley stepped aside from the problem on the board. "Okay," she said to the room of comatose eyes. Half of the students were still asleep. First hour on Mondays were the worst. "The first thing we want to do," she said, "is cancel out the like terms." She began slashing through letters and numbers on both sides of the equation. Susan yawned and did the same on her paper.

The door opened quickly; Karen ran in. Her eyes were puffy and red. She darted for Susan.

Susan sat bolt upright. "What?" she said.

Karen's hands shook. "Jen's dead," she said. "It was a drunk driver."

This isn't technically from my fiction journal; I wrote it after an idea struck one day on my way into school. It's the first piece of my fiction I show the students, so — in order to get honest feedback — I tell them it's by a famous writer named "Jeanette Thompson". Then we have fun figuring it out together.

Letter to a Young Writer

A certain ruthlessness and a sense of alienation from society is as essential to creative writing as it is to armed robbery.

Nelson Algren

First of all, get over yourself. The ego is the enemy of excellence. You will soon encounter some insight (possibly from yourself) that you will hesitate to accept, because it might contradict the notion that you are the most brilliant and clever architect of language who ever walked the Earth. If you're content to become a stagnant, bitter person, then by all means worship your own creative genius. Otherwise, as Rainer Maria Rilke is rumored to have said: "Make your ego porous." (Read Rilke's *Letters to a Young Poet*. He knows what he's talking about. While you're at it, Read Nelson Algren's *Nonconformity*, my favorite book about writing. Also read Edwidge Danticat's essay "Women Like Us" and Stephen King's *On Writing*.)

For me writing is a weird combination of passion, ecstasy, addiction, and liberation. When I can write fiction effectively, it reinforces my conviction that I can make sense of my own life. I can't tell if the narrative voice in my head is a reflection of my love for storytelling, or vice-versa, because it has always been with me. In any case, there is a deep link for me between living and writing. (Honoré de Balzac said: "If it were not for coffee, one could not write, which is to say one could not live.")

Writing fiction isn't really easy for me, but it's not fair to say it's difficult either. Some stories (like *Agoraphobia*) simply come to me, and my job is more like a stenographer than anything else. I just have to write down what I've been sent. Others (like *z*) require a good deal of sweat, toil, and uncertainty.

Even when the writing is slow and arduous, though, I love it. One reason is the sense of accomplishment. I love being able to hand people a story I've written, and — on those rare occasions when they actually read it — discuss the ideas within. Of course this is another lair of the ego. Once while I was driving to work at a bookstore in Gainesville, Florida, a sentence from a story I had read suddenly popped into my head. I spent a few minutes admiring the sentence, how well it was constructed, how effective its diction, how clever the arrangement. Then I remembered that *I* had written it.

Even if I mostly wrote crap, however, I would still do it. (And I do sometimes write crap. Every writer worth a damn knows that s/he produces work of wildly varying quality.) This is the addiction part. I've got notebooks filled with scribbles, scraps of paper covered in barely-legible story concepts, and endless computer files containing snippets of conversation. I suppose I have trouble finishing the things I start, but I don't trust people — certainly not writers — who never start things they don't finish. I think being an artistic person of integrity requires you to surround yourself with fragmented works-in-progress.

Maya Angelou said: "I always feel that I've just started. The work to be, the work that's yet to come [...] it will remain there, to be done, no matter what happens." If you don't feel this way, perhaps you aren't a writer. I say this not to stifle you, although when Flannery O'Connor was asked if she thought universities stifle writers, she supposedly said: "My opinion is that they don't stifle enough of them." (More on this below.) Rather, I don't want you to waste your time (or your reader's, especially if the reader is me) if you're not *driven* to tell the story.

Which brings me to my next piece of advice: Have a *specific* purpose for each story. Why does your story need to be told, and are you sure it hasn't been told before? (This is why you must read a lot, if you wish to write well.) If it has been told before and needs to be told again, how will your retelling be unique? Never write a story — or at least never publish it, or give it to another human — just because you feel like making up a story. (Of course this clashes with WP Mayhew's advice in *Barton Fink*, and while there's nothing wrong with escapism *per se*, there's plenty of it in the world. Meanwhile we are in desperate need of stories with substance.)

One of the most important life skills you can develop as a writer is to observe the natural flow of a good story. Tim O'Brien's *The Things They Carried* is full of this sort of thing. (That book is as much about storytelling as it is about war.) Observe this in the things you read, the movies you watch, the anecdotes you hear from friends. Become a student of story pacing; figure out when a story demands to move quickly (or slowly) and why.

Closely tied to this is the matter of human speech. If you want to write good fiction, you must absorb actual patterns of talking from the people around you. Stop mentally chastising them for pronouncing a word incorrectly and instead pay attention to which words they use and why. Tune in to their rhythms and melodies. Naturally you'll want to interact with people from many walks of life, lest your characters all sound exactly like you. But this is good advice for being a decent human, never mind your evolution as a writer.

You also need to discover your writing voice. This is nearly impossible to explain; I don't even know how I would describe my own voice, except to say that I feel comfortable with it (after many years of discomfort), and I know how to access it. This is related to the question of your unique approach mentioned above. How do you want your reader to engage with the characters and events? Is the narrator in between you and the story relevant? What emotion(s) do you want to evoke in the reader when they finish the story? Where do things like humor, didacticism, and acidity fit into your story? All of these things are elements of voice, but the only way to really uncover it is to write a lot. Eventually you'll find it.

The other thing to keep in mind is that you have a poetic license, which means that the rules you've had drilled into your head in school are void where prohibited by necessity. The only real rule in writing is to write what's true. And if it's true that you need to start a sentence with a conjunction (even though you're not supposed to), then go for it. Just make sure you know which rule you're breaking and why. This is also connected to voice, as in Patricia Powell's novel *Me Dying Trial*. The Jamaican narrator constantly says things like "I didn't mind a tall." This is incorrect according to *Warriner's English Grammar and Composition*, but it's perfect for the story she's telling.

Also remember that your head is a messy and brightly-lit place when you're writing a story. Readers, on the other hand, are in an orderly but very dark place when they come inside. They can only see what you show them, and it's easy for you to think you've made something clear when you haven't. Sometimes this can be effective and intentional — less is more, as they say, and readers like to piece some things together along the way. But when you take it too far and obfuscate for the sake of obfuscation (or if you don't realize that some things aren't illuminated for the reader), your audience will be confused and frustrated. Have someone else read your story before you make it widely available, or at least read it with fresh eyes. (Spend a week apart from it, and try to read it as if it were written by someone else.)

One last piece of advice is to pay close attention to the themes and patterns that emerge as you tell the story. You can try to plan these out, but I've had the most success with observing them unfold organically as I compose the thing. Case in point: *Agoraphobia* started out as a story about breaking out of prison. But I soon realized it had to be about twins, and then I came up with the flash drive and the bit about the murmuring just showed up in their backstory. As I worked with it, I realized the story kept returning to themes like appearance being different from reality, and people speaking quietly. You don't want to force these things into the light — if they're important, they will attract just enough attention where they are. The more subtle you are with thematic development (assuming you don't make it invisible), the more rewarding the process will be for your reader.

Think about describing a beloved movie or book to someone who hasn't seen it. At some point you've probably said: "It's about X, but it's not *really* about X." *Fight Club* isn't really about boxing, right? Of course it is, but it's *really* about the tao and the middle way, and consumption, and what it means to love other people, and living in the moment, and a dozen other things. *Macbeth* is about regicide, but it's *really* about the fragile construction of the self, and the power of social interaction, and the vagaries of prophecy. You need to approach your story in the same way. What's it *really* about?

I have a big banner in my classroom that says *WRITING LIBERATES*, and I believe this with every fiber of my being. Telling important stories can help you understand the world and your place in it better, and it might help enlighten other people too. Write what you know, be true to yourself, do the right thing, and reject mediocrity.

Good luck and have fun.

Eric S. Piotrowski
June 2013

Gratitude

Most books have a section at the end called "Acknowledgements", but that seems wildly insufficient here. (It's something a robot would say: "I acknowledge that my fembot partner has supported me. Affirmative.") Instead, here is a list of people to whom I owe a debt of gratitude.

Thank you:

- Mom and Dad, for encouraging me in everything I've done. You once gave me a program for the Apple //e called *Bank Street Writer*. It featured a Norman Rockwell-style picture of two happy parents watching their child churn out pages and pages of writing. Well, here — at last — are some of mine.

- Mark, for being the best brother ever. Thanks a lot there, bottlenose!

- Diane, for love and support and patience and joy. You make me a better person, and you make a lot of sense. Thanks also for the meticulous copyedit.

- Christie and Garrett, for always providing support and feedback on music, writing, and other stuff.

- The English department at SPHS, and especially the EyePod. Betsy, Kristi, Lisa, Kayla, Brooke, Jamie, Faith, Creed, Chris, Charlie, Deidre, Jen, MB — You rock. I couldn't ask for a better gang of comrades in these academic trenches.

- Jim and Sue and Vicki and Val and all the other teachers who have retired since I began at SPHS. Thanks for your support and wisdom.

- My students, especially those who take my class seriously and push themselves to become better writers. I hope these pages are useful and/or enjoyable. Writing liberates!

- My friends in town, especially Chris and Kelly and Heather and Julie and Tom and Inga. Also the local New College crew: Amy and Josh and Colleen and John and Doug and Liv.

- Stu and Chinny and all the VeteranGamers (and everyone on the VG Hub). I'm really fortunate to be part of such a great community. Jason!

- Megan, for being my oldest friend and providing relentless support.

- Annie and Mala, for fighting the power without sacrificing love and kindness.

- Pam and Curt and Yohan and Milena and Colleen and Hector, for continuing the fight in and for East Timor. A luta continua!

- Jesse, for being creative and awesome and supportive.

- Awadewit, Willow, Moni3, Figureskatingfan, Yllosubmarine, JayHenry, and all the other Wikipedians who have supported me and taught me about that kind of writing.

- Ron, for once chastising me for not writing more during the summer. At one point you said "That thing ain't gonna write itself." You were right, and you motivated me to get to work.

- Pat Lopez and Joan Maples for their loving support and pedagogical excellence at Buchholz High School.

Gratitude

- Douglas Langston, Andrea Dimino, Paul Buchanan, and Charles Green for their vital intellectual guidance at New College.
- Tom Bissell, for conversations about writing, history, and virtual morality. Check out his books *The Father of All Things* and *Extra Lives: Why Video Games Matter*.
- JaySmooth, for coining the term "the little hater". Check him out at illdoctrine.com.
- Julia Wertz, for telling stories well and giving me confidence to self-publish. Check out her comics memoir *The Infinite Wait*.
- Stephanie Kolodij, for the info and support via Reddit. Check out her book *Biology Doesn't Care About Your Feelings*.
- Gretchen at *A Room of One's Own* bookstore, for her kind support and assistance. Check them out at roomofonesown.com.
- All the sons and daughters of my friends, whose names I will *not* attempt to list, because I'll leave some out and feel bad. You're all very cute and awesome. Sorry for not fixing everything before you showed up. Good luck with that.
- Everyone who has ever read my stuff, especially those who have offered feedback or specific comments. I appreciate your help.
- You, for reading this. I hope my scribbling has been worth your time.

Printed in Great Britain
by Amazon.co.uk, Ltd.,
Marston Gate.